THE WOMAN WHO LOVED AIRPORTS

The Woman Who Loved Airports

*f*tories and narratives

Marusya Bociurkiw

Press Gang Publishers
Vancouver

Some of this work was previously published, as follows: "Fucking in the Air" in *Fireweed;* "The Lesbian Ocean" in *Rites;* an earlier version of "Mama, Donya" in *Fireweed,* and in *The Journey Prize Anthology* (Toronto: McLelland & Stewart, 1990); "Blue Video Night" in the anthology *Dykewords* (Toronto: Women's Press, 1990); "Courage" in *Fireweed;* and "Enemy Aliens" in *Front* magazine.

The author gratefully acknowledges financial assistance from the Ontario Arts Council Writers Reserve Program during the writing of this book.

The Publisher gratefully acknowledges financial assistance from the Canada Council and the Cultural Services Branch, Province of British Columbia.

Canadian Cataloguing in Publication Data

Bociurkiw, Marusya, 1958–
    The woman who loved airports

    ISBN 0-88974-035-6
    1. Lesbianism—Fiction. I. Title.
PS8553.O24W55 1994   C813'.54   C94-910178-8
PR9199.3.B62W55 1994

Edited by Nancy Pollak
Author photograph by Susan M. Stewart
Cover image from Marusya Bociurkiw's video, *Bodies in Trouble*
Design and typesetting by Val Speidel
Typeset in Minion
Printed and bound in Canada by Best Gagné Book Manufacturers Inc.
Printed on acid-free paper

Press Gang Publishers
101–225 East 17th Avenue
Vancouver, B.C. v5v 1A6
Canada

For the women in my extended familia, *especially*
Barb, Lesya, Neysa, Sheena and Zainub,
and for my Baba

Присвяную цю книжку усім жінкам
в моєї поширеної родини,
особливо для
Варвари, Лесі, Нейси, Шіни, Зийноб,
і для моєї Баби .

Contents

III

BODY JOURNEYS

Acknowledgements

WRITING FROM THE MARGINS requires a culture of support, so I thank the delicate but persevering network of feminist, lesbian/gay and progressive publishers, presses, journals and magazines that have given voice to feminist and lesbian literature in this country. In particular, *Rites, Fireweed* and *Fuse* were the first to publish my work on a consistent basis; their dedication to alternative writing in a time of censorship and cutbacks has been crucial to my own cultural survival. The Women's Press gave me a place to learn about writing, politics and publishing in an atmosphere of fun and solidarity; they, along with Press Gang Publishers, have nurtured my writing and exposed me to the groundbreaking work of countless other women.

I am grateful to all those who have given me feedback, editorial comment and advice. The Lesbian Writers Group of Montreal was an important circle of impassioned discussion and helpful criticism. Many friends, colleagues and lovers sat patiently through various drafts of stories and prose-poems, and their appreciative listening and reading helped me to feel connected to a larger story.

Carolyn Gammon, Ellen Jacobs, Martha Judge, Karen Knights and Anita Sheth have provided invaluable commentary over the years.

Barbara Kuhne oversaw the publishing of this book with finesse. My editor and friend Nancy Pollak deserves special mention, not only for her precision editing and great martinis, but also for kick-starting this project into production.

This collection represents several years of nocturnal writing: time snatched from the jaws of film/video making, teaching and family illness. I have been infinitely sustained by the comforting continuity, food, laughter and love of friends and family. Sheena Gourlay provided endless computer/dinner support in my pre-Macintosh years, and many scholarly insights into notions of identity and difference. Lesya Laschuk and Barbara Wisnoski were generous with hospitality, advice, recipes and delicious Ukrainian sisterhood. Leslie Stewart loved and listened through difficult times and many first drafts. Susan M. Stewart was always there with feedback, crisis intervention and author photos and, with Jaclyn Valois, gave me healing, creative space in the Kootenays of British Columbia. Beth Brant, Helen Potrebenko and Julie Vandervoort encouraged, passed on business advice and provided me with precedents. My Baba and Mama gave me language and tradition and (some of the) stories, and the strength to make up the rest. Haida Paul and Zainub Verjee welcomed me home. This book was carried through the night by these women's belief in my work.

Preface

From the Heart of Difference

YOU'RE NOT   *or you are   or you're two opposite things at once*
so that one says defiantly: write it all down   and the other whispers
secretively: don't   but you write   you keep writing   you write
from your heart   you write from your empty pockets   you write
from your anger   you write from your love   you write from your
sorrow   you write from your healing place   you write from the
centre of your opposites   and you make that a fragile home.

   You remember that, in Ukrainian, the word for writing is pysaty
and that the word for Easter Egg is pysanka: *literally, written object.*
You remember your history   a thousand years   two thousand
years   the egg is a circle, symbol of the maternal cosmos   and to
write on it is a woman's sacred task, passed from generation to gener-
ation.   To write – because with the pysanka, *each mark is a symbol*
with a specific meaning – is to continue history and to believe in
eternal life.

How does one write a story that doesn't have a single plot? How do
I write an identity that doesn't hang by a single thread?

What's your book (film/video/story/poem) about?

Lesbian identity.

Cultural location.

The gaps between theory and activism.

Breakups.

Sex.

Food.

The space between identities is the space I write from. Which is to say, there is often a lot of silence, not to mention the cracks you could fall into:

The puzzled silence of an audience that didn't get what it expected.

The contented silence of an audience that did.

The sweet silence of intimacy between lovers.

The sharp silence of cruelty between lovers.

The complacent silence of a fixed lesbian identity.

The reverberating silence of a language that exists only in your memory.

The hollow silence of a history that doesn't speak your name.

Never has it been more important for me to write from the heart of difference, towards an imaginary audience of lovers, family and friends, where languages and identities mingle freely and without contempt. I write at a time when feminism is deeply feared and difference is reviled. Those fears are being reproduced in our alternative communities and our cultures. Yet we need one another's differences – our own multiple locations – the way we need air and water and food. And we need a literature that names this; what Audre Lorde called "that safe-house of difference so necessary to change."

Because so much has gone awry. In the year this book was

conceived, huge numbers of Canadians voted for a fundamentalist right-wing party. Neo-fascists organized large and small gatherings across North America. The last independent feminist print-shop in North America closed its doors. Unemployment and welfare subsidies were cut back as never before. Immigrants and refugees are being turned back at the border in record numbers, as are lesbian, gay and feminist books, while those same borders are open wide for international trade.

Everywhere I look, there is a cry for false universals, for a patriotism that will restore a fractured Canadian (or American) identity. Of necessity, this unity must prevent the passing of messages in the night, between and across identities.

What does any of this have to do with a book of short stories? More to the point, what does writing have to do with changing any of these things, when change seems to have become a rock that does not move? During the height of the Persian Gulf War, I said to my friend Martha: "It feels so unimportant, so stupid, to be making art right now."

"That's what they want," said Martha. "They want you to forget the details."

They *want* silence.

In this strange and exciting borderland of ethnicity and gender, languages are fluid and ever-changing   the voices of mothers and grandmothers speak loudly and fiercely, translating easily into the language of the body   and art is as necessary as bread.

And so you write   then you don't   then you do again. Some things remain unspeakable and others are spoken for the first time   this, too, is political.

Pysaty: to write, to inscribe into history   to keep a cultura *alive. A very thin line on a slowly revolving egg.*

I

DEPARTURES

The Woman Who Loved
Airports

THE WOMAN WHO LOVES airports is waiting for her final boarding call. It's an important ritual for her, to be the last to board the plane. She's happy here, in this clean, pastel environment, flipping through *People* magazine, eating duty-free Belgian chocolates, spying on private, awkward spectacles of embraces and goodbyes. She's gathering material, she's conducting research, she's compiling anecdotes. Although she hates the waiting, she loves to savour the illusion of purpose that an airport Departures lounge provides.

She has been travelling for three months now, maybe more, rising into the clouds like the Blessed Virgin Mary of her childhood, then plunging like a miracle into a new city, a film tucked beneath her arm. Usually, a woman in a leather or denim jacket waits for her at the bottom of the Arrivals escalator, a complete stranger who peers closely and then tentatively utters her name. The woman who loves airports is always embarrassed at these moments of unequal recognition. She feels sheepish, as though she's been found out. Her courage sinks as she watches her anonymity float away. She becomes what she really is, a filmmaker in slightly wrinkled clothes, low in iron and cash, obediently travelling from city to city, her life's work nestled beneath her arm.

Nonetheless, the woman who loves airports is content to be travelling, always in a state of transition, swimming in the unfamiliar privilege of airports and hotels and the whiteness of her skin. Only once is she detained at customs. Why exactly is she going to San Francisco? What will she *do* there? What *precautions* will she take? She feigns innocence. After 40 minutes, she gets through.

The airports are sites of human drama, endless material for films she will not find the money or desire to do. In Chicago, waiting for a delayed flight, she meets a woman dressed in a blue crimplene pantsuit. The woman who loves airports has not seen crimplene, or pantsuits, in fifteen years, not since Anne Murray accepted the Order of Canada in one. The crimplene woman carries a sceptre. She explains that she is returning from an International Medievalist's convention in Cincinnati, where she was elected Queen via a jousting match between two knights (an Italian grocer from Brooklyn and a Canadian dentist now living in Oslo). In confidential tones, the Queen describes the coronation as the most important moment of her adult life.

In a coffee shop at the Vancouver airport, the woman who loves airports meets a certified Voyageur. He obtained his credentials by canoeing the Fraser River, from Vancouver to Prince George, in full seventeenth-century explorer's garb. He has the certificate to prove it, which he lays on the counter and smooths, reverentially. He lost his wife, she took the kids, he'd been gone eight months. But he has no regrets and keeps repeating this, shaking his head: No regrets *whatsoever.*

On an overnight flight from Toronto to Seattle, she sits next to a chatty insomniac named Ida, from Detroit. They order drinks at 3 A.M. and then Ida wants to know what the woman who loves airports does. Then she wants to know what the film's about and then, after she knows that, she wants to know whether it was difficult working with *lesbian* actors. It had been, actually, but the woman who loves airports mouths the party line and says: No, because the thing is, I'm one too. Well I'll be damned, says Ida, never tried it myself. How do you find it? Fine, how do you like being straight? Well I only sleep with drag queens, says Ida. Why's that? *Fuck if I know,* says Ida and stares out at the moon.

The woman who loves airports' ex-lover-once-removed once asked her, as she rushed to catch a plane: *What are you always running away from?* The question stayed with her, sloshed about in her thoughts like an ice cube that wouldn't melt. She wondered about being on her own, she wondered about being afraid of stillness. She wondered about so many women she knew who were doing what they wanted, which was so different from how their mothers had lived their lives. The thing was, these women all felt alone. Usually if they were, but especially if they weren't.

Now it seems that everyone she meets is running away from something, too, and that maybe airports are a way for all the avoiders and runners and escapists to connect and to figure out why.

Did you have a good flight, the women who meet her at the Arrivals escalator always ask, and then: Do you have any luggage? They walk together to the baggage area and the woman who loves airports tells an amusing story about the plane ride, to break the proverbial ice: the man who mistook her for k.d. lang, or some version of the drag-queen-fag-hag exchange. There is always an amusing story to tell, but she usually feels tired after telling it. She feels pressure to perform, to pull out snapshots, to soften the edge of privilege. To make a connecting line between the stranger's life and her own.

Flying from New York to Toronto at night, she sees specks of light everywhere, connecting up at roadways and intersections: a huge, improbable network of human existence, of unseen bridges and freeways, familiar landmarks to people she has never met. At these times, the woman who loves airports feels like a speck of light with no connecting thread. Perhaps, she rationalizes, the connecting light is her film which, unravelled, would stretch for several New York City blocks. It sometimes seems that the celluloid travels from a painful spot inside her heart and that her task is this: to rewind the spool, to pull it inward instead of outward, to recharge the pale, insubstantial speck of light.

The woman who loves airports is often asked where she's going and why. This city or that city, she says, to show my film. There is always, then, an escalation of interest, a slight leaning forward. The woman who loves airports is always afraid to disappoint these people, with their childlike yearning to be in the company of someone important. But it's such a bother to come out to people one barely knows, to utter "lesbian-and-gay-film-festival" with simulated matter-of-factness. Instead, she is vague or glib. I'm actually a complete unknown, she often says. She's telling the truth, but they think she's being coy. This is, she thinks, what it means to be part of a cultural underground.

Once, one of these airport confidantes did some research, found her event listed in the local paper and, bizarrely, unexpectedly, appeared at the screening in Edmonton – Herb, the marketing director whose camping snapshots she had been privy to over martinis in the Winnipeg airport bar. She had declined his offer of a tour of the West Edmonton Mall and they had parted at the baggage carousels, on amicable terms.

She showed her film that night: feature-length, with long, unedited and oddly unerotic scenes of lesbians thrashing in bed,

complex dialogues about lesbian-feminist theories of spectatorship, and no plot. Her work met with bewildered applause, fol-
lowed by the obligatory and awkward question-and-answer period. She scanned the audience for a face that didn't look bored,
hostile or simply indifferent, and there was Herb – flushed, grinning, his arm in the air. A brash young gym teacher was chairing
the proceedings and knew enough to ignore Herb. But there
weren't enough questions to fill the void – in fact, there weren't
any – and Herb wasn't lowering his arm. He stood up, slowly and
deliberately, buttoned his jacket and straightened his tie: I want to
thank you for sharing this movie with us. I got a very clear picture
of how difficult and tragic it is to have been born homosexual in
this day-and-age. But what I wanted to know is, *why do you despise
men so much?*

The gym teacher broadjumped to the mike and announced they
were unfortunately out of time. Herb was the first to float up to the
woman who loves airports, to take her hand in both of his and,
beaming, to congratulate her on her 'talent' and 'courage.' When
she pulled away, a piece of paper with the phone number of his
hotel room lay crumpled in her palm.

The woman who loves airports has sent 23 postcards from eleven
different cities in the past four months. She describes the funny
things that happen to her, without mentioning either her isolation
or her fatigue. The recipients of the postcards are working in battered women's shelters or bankrupt women's bookstores, or sitting
in tense collective meetings, or waitressing in fern cafés. They are
making more money than her and she is staying in more hotels
than they ever have. It is a complicated irony. She will return, unable to connect her experience to theirs.

She has introduced her film fifteen times and each time, she has slightly less to say. In the dry southern city, she finds herself at a champagne reception, standing next to The Famous Gay Film-maker From Britain. He is surrounded by a respectful knot of people clasping drinks, while he describes his impressions of the North American lesbian and gay movement. He expresses his concern for *gender essentialism*: that tired old fixation on lesbian feminism, its anti-porn hysteria, its distance from the major discourses on representation.

The woman who loves airports – Canadian, daughter of immigrants – has an ancestral distaste for British imperialism and she's always been allergic to misogyny. But she has drunk too much champagne. She blurts: *Now wait one second. There are many different kinds of feminism, you know. . . .*

A silence spreads around her. The imprint of her voice lingers in this grudging space, tenuous and uncertain. She wants to say more, but can't. The Famous Gay Filmmaker permits himself a smile. The Harried Festival Organizer rushes to freshen The Famous Gay Filmmaker's drink. The Tweedy Gay Intellectual looks at The Famous Gay Filmmaker and raises one eyebrow. The Important Film Critic laughs, shrugs and walks away.

She begins to feel like a warrior whose armour was lost with her luggage, a comedian who misplaced her humour suitcase, a lone feminist on a battleship out at sea. You'd never know there was a war going on: palm trees fill the room, there is soft music and hors d'oeuvres, and all the men are gay. She suddenly understands what her ex-lover-once-removed once said to her, on the way to the airport: *Be careful, honey. These days, feminism is the scariest thing around.*

Two hours later, the woman who loves airports is introducing the film to an audience of 1,000 people. The champagne reception was, in fact, partly in honour of the film's premiere. The Famous

Gay Filmmaker has apologetically slipped away for dinner, entourage in tow, leaving her alone with Debbie, the painfully shy volunteer. I don't know why they gave me this job, said Debbie, *I'm painfully shy.* Debbie has been assigned to her for the evening and Debbie is faithful, smiles brightly from her first row seat and makes a thumbs-up sign.

The woman who loves airports has left her body. Her soul, flying somewhere above, is exquisitely light with pleasure and relief, defying gravity and despair. Her body, in the meantime, sweats. It wants to pee, it wants to go home, it wants to disappear.

Later, after her soul has reunited with her body, she cannot for the life of her remember what she said to the audience. But she knows there were waves of energy and humour that were as good as sex. And there were 1,000 people gathered to see the film she almost broke her heart completing.

The rest of the evening is composed of innumerable particles of light. A woman saying to her: Your film gives me hope. Crowds of dykes on the street outside the cinema, illuminated in the pink neon glow of the marquee. A late dinner with a group of other lesbian filmmakers, hastily assembled by The Harried Festival Organizer. A post-structuralist critic from France, who gives her a ride to the restaurant on her motorcycle. Long, delicious gulps of laughter, later, at the bar.

She dances till 3 A.M. with Debbie, whose shyness has lapsed, and the post-structuralist, whose name she never remembers. The Famous Gay Filmmaker and his entourage join them. They have decided, for that night, to be her friends.

Three months later, the woman who awaits her at the Arrivals escalator in the cold northern city is tall, with spiky grey hair, a black leather jacket and a wide, shy smile. Hello, I'm the token lesbian on the film festival committee, she says by way of welcome. The woman who loves airports, slightly shaky from two months of consecutive festivals and strangers, had been determined to go immediately to her hotel where she would stay, watching soap operas, until her screening. Instead, she accepts this woman's halting offer of lunch and sits for two hours in a hanging fern café, eating fusilli and watching this woman's elliptical mouth form itself around notions of cinematic theory, lesbian culture and life in a small provincial town. She holds onto the edge of the faux marble table, dizzy with the sudden panorama of this woman and, also, with lack of sleep.

Her position in regard to those who meet her at the Arrivals escalator is not uncomplicated. There is the fact of absence and of need, and of the welcoming space provided for lesbian images, no matter what those images are. There is the false importance attached to artists, which is simply the reverse of the actual unimportance of art to most people's lives. And there is the minor reputation that precedes her: the article in the feminist newspaper where her name was spectacularly misspelled, seven different ways; and the photograph in her press package, out of date by four years, depicting her joyously shouldering a camera (she never does her own camera work anymore), seemingly immune to burnout or bankruptcy.

You don't look at all like your photograph, says the grey-haired woman in the fern café.

That night, the woman who loves airports screens her film to the cold northern audience of people who never take off their jackets, though the cinema is warm. Almost everyone sneaks out during the final credits and no one stays for discussion. The grey-haired festival organizer is apologetic, but reassures her: No one discusses anything here anymore.

They repair to a drag queen bar in a deserted area of this cold northern city, where they find themselves with three other patrons, reluctantly watching a floor show: a seven-foot-tall white fag, pretending to be Tina Turner. It is a Tuesday night, 2 A.M. The woman who loves airports and the grey-haired festival organizer have run out of things to say. Conversation is not the point here, anyway. Their bodies brush against each other, lean towards each other, ache.

After all the re-writes, the struggles with her computer, the humiliations of fundraising, the sheer desperate isolation of the second draft, the stage fright of the actors, the manic depression of the sound recordist, the attenuated boredom of the final sound mix, and the diplomatic intricacies of airport exchanges – after all that, it comes down to this: the over-arching desire to connect with another woman's body, to draw a line of light.

She explains to the grey-haired woman in the early morning hours: It's not that I don't appreciate all this travelling, all this being able to speak. But I didn't realize how dangerous it could be.

They don't make love, in the end. They talk until the sun comes up and they don't get tired. They've recognized each other.

And truth, which is not the same thing as always trying to be positive, always trying to be *nice*, turns out to be a powerful thing.

The woman who loves airports is in the air again, on her way home. At the L.A. airport, she meets a psychic who tells her she will find great happiness and a monogamous relationship – in about ten years. Changing flights, she finds herself once again in the Chicago airport and realizes it's August. Dusty women with backpacks and vulva necklaces grin at her from adjacent moving walkways. In the line-up to the security area, she exchanges pleasantries with a majorette troupe from Washington, whose batons have been wreaking havoc in the x-ray machine. She worries about her vibrator. She feels a fleeting sense of community, of being on the edge and belonging to that edge.

Relief and loss flicker through her. The relief is about going home, about imagining the ironic, smiling face of her ex-lover-once-removed at the bottom of the Arrivals escalator. The loss is about her audience, which has dispersed and no longer exists, which didn't really see itself as her audience anyway. Was maybe just a bunch of people going to a movie. She thinks, wistfully, that she never got to know this audience, never got to see the other end of the line of celluloid unravelling from her heart.

The day is clear. The plane seems to be flying low, but it's just an illusion created by the lack of clouds. The woman who loves airports sees lakes, shining dully like platinum, and sectioned-off fields, tiny perfect barns, ragged forests and occasionally, pale blue mountains. The world looks as ordinary and orderly as a Fisher-Price toy. The interior of the airplane reproduces this effect. Airline attendants in crisp white blouses and bright crayon lipstick dispense stiff drinks. The woman who loves airports sips her scotch and soda and silently toasts the grey-haired festival organizer. She reins in her soul, which had been flying dangerously low, and holds it inside her body.

She's reeling back the celluloid, winding energy back into the light. The light is being repossessed; hers now, turning inward: a speck of light with frail, connecting threads.

Fucking in the Air

EVERY WOMAN I'd ever slept with showed up in Vancouver for the Gay Games. It was an accident, of course, but my best friend Giselle couldn't help but wonder: "Imagine if they all met for lunch. . . . "

It was August. Sunlight ricochetted from ocean to pavement and up into our skins. I got an eye infection, I had trouble seeing. I was dazzled by the light and by the sight of so many lesbians. I was very nervous and needed to take a lot of coffee breaks. My friend Jamie reassured me in her wisecracking way.

"Don't worry, girlfriend. Soon, things will be back to normal and all the lesbians will be invisible again."

Jamie was a jock. We slept together once, on the coldest night of the year. February. It was so cold you instantly got an icecream headache when you went outside. Despite, or perhaps because of this, the women's bars were full every night.

Jamie and I were coming home from Café Sappho that extremely cold evening. I didn't have mittens.

"Come to my house," said Jamie. "I have extra mittens." We

were right in front of my house as she made this generous offer. That should have been a warning: Jamie definitely did not know how to express desire.

The Gay Games began with a huge opening ceremony. The Lesbian and Gay Freedom Bands of America, resplendent in sequins, stars, stripes and batons, marched around a huge stadium that had been built by developers' money off the backs of Vancouver's homeless. I sat in the stands with my girlfriend and about 20,000 other queers. With great bravado, I put one arm around her shoulder and drank beer with the other. I cheered and hooted along with everyone else. I said to my girlfriend: "I feel normal!" It was a joke, of course, and she laughed in her indulgent way while her body braced itself against my sarcasm. Silently, I wondered whose freedom we were celebrating, in a country that had long ago been occupied by America. I rubbed my girlfriend's back and tried to see the ceremony through her cool blue Scottish eyes. For a moment, I saw 20,000 queers feeling good about themselves and pretending to be normal, in a campy sort of way. When Jamie marched in with the Ontario contingent – which was only about a quarter of the size of the Ohio contingent – I cheered again.

Jamie had been agile. She had wrapped her legs around my stomach, licked my thighs and tickled my toes, all at the same time. As she fell asleep, she whispered something that was simultaneously feminist in spirit and sexy in attitude, something about how effective the anti-free trade demo had been; something about getting so wet at seeing me there, it had shown through her pants. Jamie was versatile, but she could never say she wanted me. She necked with me quite pleasantly after Coalition Against Economic Repression meetings. She played footsie with me during the benefit for striking Eaton's workers. I invited her to my apartment after a Lesbians for Choice meeting. She shrugged and said maybe. She never let me into her bed again.

The coalition disbanded. The Eaton's strikers were forced back to work. We got our free-standing abortion clinic. And Jamie and I didn't see each other for a year and a half.

Even though I was on holiday, I set my alarm clock each morning for 7 A.M. so I wouldn't miss anything. There were: queer movies and dyke softball and sex videos and poetry readings and impromptu baton-twirling parades. There were: drag queens lounging in yuppie sidewalk cafés, lesbians buying peaches and take-out coffee at Portuguese corner stores, and fags who had never met before, sitting together in the backs of buses and laughing loudly.

Taking some time out, my girlfriend and I went to an aquarium on the other side of town to see the dolphins. There were at least nine other lesbians there, peering into the pale turquoise water. We saw two women necking in front of the shark tank, their heads surrounded by an aura of transient blue light.

My girlfriend and I got very tired and quarrelled on the way home. I don't know if it was because of the long hours, the sensory overload, or because we were running into every woman I'd ever slept with in my life.

I saw Mercurie out of the corner of my eye, at the delicatessen on Commercial Drive. She was buying chorizo. I guessed she wasn't vegetarian anymore, but I couldn't ask her because we weren't speaking. Mercurie was a performance artist. She was most renowned for her lesbian three-ring circus, a metaphor for non-monogamy which featured trapeze artists who fucked in the air. Through the grapevine, Mercurie had heard I had been on an arts council jury that had denied her funding. I hadn't, but somehow we let the grapevine speak for us with its twisting, menacing tendrils. One day, we made an appointment through our phone machines to meet at Café Sappho and straighten things out. Mercurie never showed up.

Mercurie had been rough and clever in bed, biting, wrestling and laughing. It was a summer affair. Our skin sweated into each other's pores. She was very straightforward, said she didn't want a relationship, insisted we use latex and never looked me in the eye when we made love.

When we first met, we had dates and discussions about art, and long luxurious phone calls.

"I've grown fond of you," Mercurie said. We began to be friends and then we fell into bed. Our friendship became a fragile thing.

"Just say hello and get it over with," said my girlfriend wearily, as we ordered salmon pâté at the deli. My girlfriend shielded me from Mercurie with her large, solid body. I didn't say hello, but my body leaned in that direction, remembering the porousness of her. It was dark and cool among the cheeses and rows of briny olive bins. I felt oddly aroused. I wanted to lick the salty sweat from my girlfriend's neck. Outside, the heat and the lesbians blazed.

Mercurie bought two pounds of chorizo and some chicken breasts, then glanced my way. She walked over to where I was and hugged me in a matter-of-fact way, without looking me in the eye. Then she left.

Later that day, as we watched a lesbian bowling competition, my girlfriend looked me in the eye and said: "Why do you keep having people in your life who aren't there?"

"I dunno," I said. "Maybe at this point, it's a pattern that's impossible to break." I looked back into my girlfriend's eyes, which were wise and worried and had turned almost grey in the dim light of the bowling alley. I saw that she was there in a big, quiet sort of way.

The next morning we went out for breakfast on Hastings Street, to the most obscure and unlikely greasyspoon in the city, so that we could have some quality time alone. There was a line-up of lesbians at the door, trying to be alone too. We were seated at a table for four. Elena was there, with her new lover Cindy. My girlfriend sighed and buried herself in the menu.

Elena and I had had a most passionate and unexpected eight-month affair. We met at a Committee Against Racism meeting. People always asked us where we met, because they were surprised to see us together. Taxi drivers and feminists were always asking Elena where she was *from,* and then they would dispute her answer. So she started to make things up. Sweden, she would say, or Switzerland or Siberia. She would throw me a look that flashed with amusement and anger.

When I first met Elena, I talked about racism all the time, clipped articles out of the newspaper, re-read Angela Davis. I thought it was the appropriate thing to do. One morning, as I was reading aloud from an article on aboriginal land claims, Elena put down her section of the newspaper, turned to me and said: "Shut up."

"I beg your pardon?" I said.

"If I want to hear about racism I'll ask, okay?"

Our sex got better and better as we drifted apart. The more we argued, the more we came. Then, we let each other go.

I hadn't seen Elena in a year. We kissed each other on the cheek. My girlfriend hummed nervously, reading the menu like it was *War and Peace.* Cindy played with her hair. We were all introduced and shook one another's hands stiffly, like diplomats at the UN. Halfway through her scrambled eggs, Elena secretly wrapped her legs around mine. I curled my toes around her ankles. We all made polite conversation and then we left.

Out on the hot pavement, my girlfriend said to me: "I don't

want to meet any more of your ex-girlfriends. It makes me upset. I think about the kind of sex you had and whether it was as good as the sex we have. And it makes me sad to think that maybe someday I'll be your ex-girlfriend too. It makes me hurt to think that our bodies could be so close and then so far away. So please, don't introduce me to any more of your ex-girlfriends."

That afternoon, my girlfriend went to see the lesbian softball competition and I went to a queer writing workshop. When we met up later, we had completely different things to describe.

My girlfriend told me how, from a distance, the playing field looked like any other playing field. But as she got closer she could see a woman she knew who had been kicked out of her government job for being a lesbian, standing confidently at the bat. A closeted Olympic swimmer was pitching. She was competing in a sport that wasn't her specialty, so she wouldn't have an unfair advantage. A woman my girlfriend knew from highschool – Mindy, the head cheerleader – was playing left field, catching a fly ball that won the game. My girlfriend sat in the bleachers all afternoon eating hotdogs and watching lesbians flex their arms and stretch their bodies in the sun. Some of them were showing off, but that was okay. My girlfriend was there to watch, and the freedom to look was part of what the Games were all about.

I told my girlfriend about the workshop, conducted by one of my favourite lesbian writers. Although her stories were full of complicated pain, she herself was gentle and soft-spoken. I told my girlfriend how the workshop included both men and women, and how, at one point, we were talking about memory. The men talked about memory as something to do with writing technique. The women talked about memory as something to do with abuse. Haltingly and gracefully, several women spoke about how memory had surfaced in their writing and as they spoke, the men became silent and rapt. Some women, including me, read stories. I had never read a story to strangers before.

My girlfriend and I looked at each other with happy faces. We had each, separately, had such wonderful afternoons.

That evening we met up with Giselle and her lover Nadya for dinner at the dyke-run vegan café. Nicola was with them. Except that now everyone called her 'Nick' and I didn't feel like I could ask why.

I had met Nicola at some conference. I couldn't remember if it was the Feminism and the State conference, the Forum on Women and Pleasure, or the one called Chicks 'n Flicks: A Dialogue on Cinematic Representation. This was back in the days when the state still funded women's conferences. I was presenting a paper on lesbian cinema. Nicola had seen my photograph in the conference brochure and decided she wanted to meet me. She arranged to be the person who picked me up at the airport.

It was the most marvellously flattering affair. Nicola drove me around town in an old green Mercedes borrowed from a friend and took me to an amusement park. We ate pogo sticks and looked at prize cows. We had brilliant, amusing conversation. We made out on a ferris wheel and barely made it back into town for my panel that evening.

For five days, we talked about lesbian/feminist theory, then we had sex, then we ate, then talked, then had sex again. Then I had to go back. We wrote letters, then we wrote postcards. We did lunch when we were in each other's cities. We were friends, then friendly colleagues.

But at dinner, Nicola was brittle and distant.

"What's Nick all tensed up about?" asked Nadya while Nicola was in the can. Giselle shrugged innocently. My girlfriend sighed her deep, meaningful sigh. And I felt a chill wind of something halfway between grace and disgrace, something there was hardly language to describe.

I had had the gift of Nicola's friendship, then I didn't. Nothing had happened, really. The gift had simply been withdrawn.

We passed around tofu kebabs and garbanzo pâté. I tried Nadya's noodle kugel. Giselle kept taking big bites out of my sundried tomato filo pie. My girlfriend poured more wine into Nicola's glass. I asked her about her work at the women's counselling collective.

"We're underfunded, I'm overextended and I never discuss work after hours," she snapped, reaching for the yeast-free bread-sticks while I swallowed hard on my eggplant scallopini.

There was nothing to say. Nicola was burnt out. I was leaving town in four days. As I dug into my girlfriend's non-dairy carob cheesecake, I mused that the compassion, or maybe even the ethics, that would pin things down and make everyone more con-siderate didn't yet exist. Nicola had nothing to give and nothing to make her try. It was all very logical, but it didn't feel decent and it didn't feel kind.

In the days following, I went to a lesbian re-make of a fairy tale, saw fags from Texas square-dancing on the street, and drank cap-puccinos in a pool hall that was full of an equal number of Italian men and dykes. I also ran into Kate, and Gina, and Premila, and Lisette. They were ex-lovers, too. Sometimes we smiled ruefully at one another, sometimes we avoided one another. The avoiding al-ways hurt and never really seemed worth the trouble. Occasional-ly, and with great courage, we would embrace and look into one another's eyes.

The last night of the Games, my girlfriend and I went to a huge outdoor women's dance. Two women from South Carolina, wear-ing silk cowboy shirts, played guitar and fiddle for a while. They were very serious and very good.

"I don't know how many of you ladies like country music or know how to dance the two-step," one of them drawled, "but we'd sure like to encourage you-all to give it a try."

A huge cheer went up from the crowd. My girlfriend and I danced the two-step and then we just danced close together in the standard, sleazy bar-dyke way. We were remembering the imprint of each other's bodies, for the next time.

Later we sat in the bleachers, feeling sweaty and content, watching muscular women and ordinary-looking women dance or cruise or just stroll around. I saw Elena leaning against the bar, her long dark hair loose on her shoulders, looking very butch and very vulnerable. Nicola walked by wearing a cowboy hat and gave me a flashy cowgirl smile. Jamie sat with us for a while, looking nervous and fresh in her spiky streaked blonde haircut. She shook my girlfriend's hand. They looked like Martina Navratilova and Steffi Graff at the end of a tennis match.

Mercurie danced sexily with another woman, showing off some New York avant-garde-dyke dance moves. She didn't look at me at all.

But I knew we were aware of each other. I knew our bodies all remembered one another, because there were scars and new knowledge and old pain. There were the body-memories of something beyond skin, of moments of closeness that were scary to hold onto, but were all we had.

I felt sad about the scars. I felt like one of Mercurie's trapeze artists: fucking in the air. No safety net, just a casual, makeshift community, figuring out the rules as it went along. The price you paid for all that freedom was that hardly anything permanent remained.

But it was beautiful, to be able to fly like that.

The Lesbian Ocean

The numbing regularity of waves rolling in from the open Pacific hides an important fact: no two waves are identical.

ROSEMARY NEERING, The Coast of British Columbia

FROM FAR ACROSS the room I watch *her* moving on the dance floor: confident, graceful, tough, her eyes surveying the room and only occasionally colliding with mine.

I'm dancing with Benita, a friend who dropped out of public view during an obsessively monogamous five-year relationship. Recently dumped, Benita appears at dances again, fish returned to water, trying to re-acclimatize herself to the tides, the habitat, the mating rituals of this corner of the lesbian ocean. Benita surveys the crowd constantly as she dances, her mouth slightly open, her eyes at once feverish and afraid. Intermittently, she throws me coy affectionate glances and plants suggestive little touches on my bum.

Women who have just broken up constantly approach me for

advice, sex or both. Seasoned practitioner of one-night stands that I am, I must seem like a protective shoal to these nervous fishes-out-of-water. But the truth, if they only knew it, is that I'm having monogamy fantasies. And I haven't slept with anyone in over six months. Six months and three days to be exact.

As the song finally ends, I float gently but firmly out of Benita's by now overtly sexual embrace. I need a break from the waves of sexual energy and confusion that roll through the room from all directions. And, I need to strategize around making some kind of connection with *her*.

In the line-up to the washroom, two women in front are engaged in fervent discussion. I move closer.

"I've been thinking about it all week and I'm still not certain what to do. Suzanne says do something, anything, but I just don't know...."

"You've got to do what you think is right. Suzanne will understand, whatever you decide."

"But what if it doesn't work out? She could leave me!"

"Look, honey, it's like anything else. You risk getting wet, but you can pull out at any time."

I'm not exactly sure if they're discussing fist-fucking or a bank heist. Then, as the conversation turns to blue chips, safe investments and Dow averages, I realize they are working through their personal socio-economic response to the stock market crash.

I stand back and look more carefully. One woman is wearing exquisitely soft leather Danier pants with a designer cowgirl shirt, the other a black raw silk Armani suit. Their outfits combined could pay my rent, my groceries and my hydro bill for several months. I ponder this question: are these my sisters or does the class war rage on, even in the lesbian ocean?

I decide I need another diversion. The line-up, which is really just a social alternative to the dance floor, is glacially slow. I turn around and watch with shock as she enters the room. She nods perfunctorily to Armani Woman (an ex-lover, perhaps?) and then eyes me appraisingly. I fall into the shivery abyss of her grey-green eyes.

She smiles.

"*Salut*," says my desired one in a deep voice and a Québécois accent.

"Oh. Umm . . . hi," I gasp and continue to stare.

"Do I know you?" she enquires pleasantly enough, offering me a Gauloise and then lighting it.

"No! I mean, ah, no, . . . " I gasp, reduced to a coughing mess after a single inhalation of this *très chic* cigarette.

She pats my back jovially.

"Well, you never know. So many dances, so many women. . . . " She pauses in mid-sentence, as though unsure how the expression ends and shrugs, elegantly.

She turns to chat with someone who has joined the line. I pause to reflect on this outpouring of nouns and qualifiers from the object of my desire, and look bashfully at the floor. The debris of endless community events litters the black and white linoleum: abortion rally leaflets, ticket stubs, Zig Zag rolling papers, and the occasional beer bottle and animal rights petition.

Suddenly, a hand gently touches my hip. I turn reluctantly, anticipating an ever-more-persistent Benita, but it's *her*, smiling.

"*Voilà*, I think the toilet is free."

Like Persephone fleeing Hades, I sprint into the cubicle, relieved to be liberated from the amused scrutiny of my lusted-after one. I try to think. Contact has occurred sooner than expected and I don't have a plan. Her voice interrupts the chaos of my thoughts.

"Hey, any toilet paper on your side?"

"Oh, yeah, lots, plenty to spare!" I shriek.

"*Parfait....*"

Her hand appears, beckoning, beneath the wall. Slow-motion, I pass over a wad. Slow-motion, her hand lingers against mine and then disappears.

I may have made a lot of mistakes in my life, but there's one thing I know when I see it: flirtation. A cloudy, vaseline-on-the-lens image of us gliding out of our cubicles and into each other's lives plays itself out on the Cineplex Odeon screen in my head. Tousling my hair, pulling up the collar of my shirt, I swagger out of my booth.

She's gone.

Back on the dance floor, all is as it should be. Couples form and re-form, tragedy and romance play themselves out. Women of all shapes and sizes dance, giggle, flirt or skilfully avoid one another. Beside me, amid great hilarity, the entire Anarcha-Feminist Collective attempts to dance cheek-to-cheek. Nearby, Benita dances, alone, like a bird released from captivity, happy and loose. Beside her are Sumira and Andrea, who met half an hour ago (I introduced them) and are now engaged in what appears to be the act of swallowing each other's mouths. Further away, an ex-lover, Chrystyna, casts sharp, curious glances my way, her head resting on the shoulder of Astarte, another ex-lover (known, at the time, as Sally). I introduced them, too.

But she is nowhere to be seen. *Damn these cavernous Masonic temples,* I think, making my way to where Maya, an old friend from peacenik days, is sitting. Chin in hand, she watches the ever-more-furious tides of lesbian energy, with a calm bemused smile. Veteran of about 500 affairs, Maya knows more about the depraved inner goings-on of this community than even the feminist therapists do. If this were the fourth century, Maya would be a soothsayer. If this were a cop show, Maya would be an undercover double-agent. I figure she'll be able to help me.

"Hey, Maya, listen. I need some background on this woman I've been cruising. I don't know her name, but she's francophone, about five-four, short dark hair, slightly femmy. . . . "

"Green eyes?"

"Yeah, amazing green eyes."

Maya mentally searches her all-girl data-base and pulls up a file.

"Oh, yeah, I know who you mean. Slept with her in . . . let's see, 1981 or so. Just after the big disarmament rally in New York, you remember the one. I was marching with the Perverts for Peace contingent and she joined in for a while. She had been shopping and was kind of miffed that we had blocked Fifth Avenue. So anyways, I got her stoned at the rally in Central Park and helped her carry her shopping bags home. And the rest, as they say, is her-story. . . . "

"So what's she like?"

"Well, as I recall, she was really nice. Polite, good table manners. . . . "

"*Maya.*"

" . . . an absolute tiger in bed, likes to wrestle, great lingerie, not very political, but that was, what, ten years ago. . . . Hey, there she is. Hey, she's looking at you!"

And I look back at her. For a moment, we are equals, sexual power meeting its magnetic opposite from either side of the room. Her hands are in her pockets, her hips sway slightly to the music. She looks dreamy or bored, I can't tell which, but she looks at me and I look back. I look and I smile, coyly. I am a predator and this is the jungle. I am Lesbian and this is My Ocean. I am Woman and. . . .

I can't keep it up. I turn to Maya to bum a cigarette.

"Wow," says Maya. Even she is impressed.

I look up again and there she is, again. In a passionate embrace with Armani Woman.

"Oops, I guess she's still with Sandy. They've been together for forever. They own a condo at Harbourfront and play the real estate market, buy up old houses, kick out people who've been living in them for years and then sell them to rich couples. Sandy comes from old money or something and Suzanne's been a stockbroker for years. It's ironic, really, when you think of the hovels we live in, apt to be evicted at any moment by people like Sandy and Suzanne and here we are, one big happy dyke family. Oh well, live and let live, I always say. But anyways, they're non-monogamous, or so Suzanne tells me, and she's really cute. I say, go for it. . . . ."

As Maya launches into her dissertation on the relative merits of non-monogamy, I am saved by Benita, who fairly yanks me onto the dance floor, her eyes ablaze.

"You'll never believe it! I just asked a complete stranger to dance!"

"Did she accept your generous offer?" I manage to ask.

"Well, no. She muttered something about hating Madonna and that she had just come out. So I said to her, 'Look, don't sweat it. After about a year of Top 40 music at women's dances, you'll lose your musical taste buds completely, you'll dance to anything.' Well, it turns out she's, like, an experimental musician, plays with a band called the Dead Virginia Woolves. She said she needed to be alone."

"Oh well, if ya don't cruise, ya lose," I mutter despondently.

"Hey, girlfriend, can't you be a little more supportive? Why only one month ago I was sitting at home on Saturday nights, reading Ikea catalogues with Sarah, discussing vertical blinds and duvet designs, creating complicated pasta sauces and reading self-help books on Lesbian Bed Death."

I tell her about Suzanne and Sandy, and how differently the stock market crash affects us all. Benita envelops me in a sisterly embrace and we sway to Patsy Cline.

"Hey, girlfriend," she whispers in my ear. "Whaddya say we go back to my pad for some hot . . . popcorn and a late movie or two?"

Fifteen minutes later we are on the streetcar, passionately debating supply-side economics, love, sex and Madonna, along with Maya who, stood up by her date, has invited herself along. I sit back for a moment and gaze at their faces, alive with humour and courage: my fellow swimmers heading, momentarily, for the safety of the shore.

Here Nor There

BRITTA WAS bald. She had small breasts and large hands. When she touched Katya, it was with her whole palm, firmly, along the side of Katya's face, or the inside of her thighs. Katya would go to Britta's tiny Berlin apartment in Kreuzberg for short intervals and at odd times: three in the morning or two in the afternoon, between Britta's bartending shifts at Oranienbar, where she passed as a man, and her waitressing shifts at the women's café, where she passed as a vegetarian.

Britta was into genderfuck and drama.

"I like it when these guys flirt with me," she told Katya. "I let them do it and then, at the crucial moment, I turn it around and say, 'Hey, look you've got the wrong idea.'"

Just hearing about it made Katya wet.

Britta kept all her clothes on when she and Katya fucked. Katya could touch, but not see, Britta's pear-shaped breasts. Only her bald head, exposed and tender. Britta would let Katya climb on top of her and then would flip her over. Katya's breath was taken away.

Man's face on a woman's body. What was it exactly that Katya was attracted to?

And *that* was the question.

Manon has hips that sway when she walks and long dark hair that smells like sandalwood and falls onto Katya's face when they sleep. Manon is always at the airport when Katya returns from her trips away, standing on the platform high above Customs, sandwiched between large European families and lone waving wives. Every time, a different token or gesture so she'll be recognized: lavender balloons, a bouquet of latex gloves, or pink confetti (this got her taken in for questioning). Manon wears her black wide-brimmed hat and her Italian leather jacket, with her red come-fuck-me lipstick and her shiny brown cowboy boots. Katya feels a sharp stab of desire. The memory of Britta drifts into another part of her body.

Once, after the long drive back to Montreal, Manon cried as Katya touched her face firmly, with her whole hand.

"You've never touched me that way before," she said, *"qu'est-ce qui se passe?"*

Katya was frustrated, to say the least.

I dreamed you had a cock, it reached across the bed, then it was a snake, circling me, holding me so tight I could hardly breathe.

At night, Katya dreamed about Britta; in the daytime, she wrote letters to Manon.

Your touch wanders along the inside of my skin. Your voice haunts my throat. I want my eyes to be your eyes. I imagine my head between your breasts, I smell your hair, even when I'm thousands of miles away.

Her letters were all honesty and all lies.

Buoyed by an academic grant, Katya travelled to Germany frequently to do research for her Ph.D. thesis on lesbian culture in pre-war Berlin. She was conducting interviews with older German women, asking them about women's cabarets and journals, lesbian movie stars and love stories. But when she played her tapes back, she found that all anybody really wanted to talk about was the changes since the Wall went down.

"It was something to fight against, something to organize around," said Birgit, the lesbian poet from the East. "Now, it's gone, almost without a trace, and it is the same with our movements, our lesbian groups, many of our feminist organizations – *kaput,* since the Wall went down. We have less funding now, that's one thing. And also we're tired, from overwork, since everything costs so much more.

"But it's something else, too. It is as though energy comes from being contained within boundaries, even if it's a boundary you don't really choose."

Katya didn't really understand any of this at the time. After she met Britta, she lost track of her project and also of herself.

Britta consumed Katya, demanded all her attention, held Katya's head tightly between her hands and looked forcefully into her eyes. When they weren't having sex and Britta wasn't working, they'd get together with Britta's crazy friends, Utta and Marion, deejays at one of the fly-by-night women's bars, getting women to dance to something besides techno music: Salt 'n Peppa or Nina Hagen. Huddled together in the music booth, they'd take Ecstasy and then set off on marathon bar and café tours, hurtling between the East and the West on the U-bahn and in cabs.

One night, it was just Katya and Britta. They went to the Globus Bar in East Berlin and danced to techno until 9 A.M. After breakfast at the anarchist café, they wandered over to the Turkish baths to freshen up. Britta was too tired to act tough. She poured warm water over Katya and tenderly washed Katya's breasts, her arms, her stomach. She was motherly, in a way Katya had never seen a butch be motherly before.

At these times, it was impossible for Katya to write letters to Manon. So she invented a system: she would write ten postcards all at once, at the beginning of her trip, and then mail one each day.

It's beautiful here. The roses along the canal are in full bloom and there are huge oak trees bent over the café where I write. This week, I will meet with a video artist from the East, to find out about her latest project: an exposé of lesbian culture in East Germany, covering the past 60 years.

Britta took Katya on long walks to her favourite spots. Not shady places by the canal, not the sweet café courtyards, but industrial wastelands: bare spaces where the Wall once stood, abandoned factory buildings overgrown with wildflowers. Places that were once on the other side of the Wall and had been inaccessible to Britta, even though they were a kilometre or less from her apartment. For Britta, it was like having a whole new country to explore.

"Listen," she said. "Listen to the sounds."

Katya listened. Nothing out of the ordinary: a few kids playing soccer and screaming at the top of their lungs. Two young mothers chatting quietly as they bumpily pushed their baby strollers along a gravel path. Some crickets. A dog barking.

"It was completely quiet here before," said Britta.

Britta and Katya fucked on the grass of an empty field, while trains bound for Moscow whistled past.

Long walks up Mount Royal, conversation moving in and out of French and English, Katya and Manon find each other again, first through language and only then through their bodies. Discreet, sensual, sitting outside Bar Sortie, their knees touching slightly, Manon hating public displays of affection. Long periods of no talking, an assumed peaceableness that is really the reverse of the war zone in Manon's mind, the harried border crossings in Katya's heart.

I dreamed about your tight hard body last night and you saying: "Meine liebe, *give it to me, give it all to me,*" *and in my sleep, my body ached and I came till I cried.*

Manon and Katya have been together for two years, but Manon never tells Katya about her jealousy. These days, she imagines shards of glass, they slice into her sleep, they hover over her stomach while Katya is in Europe. She lies in bed and imagines Katya's arms around her, then the image changes, goes out of control: she imagines Katya and Britta together, with all the details of their fucking, a self-generated film she can spend hours unreeling. Then the feel of the glass in her stomach, up through her heart and finally, resting menacingly in her throat.

Katya checks in with her: How are you feeling, do we need to talk. Manon, always sweet, kisses Katya tenderly on the cheek and says: "*Ne t'inquiète pas,* I love you still."

Manon has only lived in Montreal, has never travelled anywhere, except to the Laurentians where her mother now lives. Once, she and Katya planned a trip to San Francisco. Manon borrowed a pile of books from the library, boned up on the history, planned some visits to museums and a walking tour. The trip was cancelled; Katya's lecture fell through. And Manon was left holding onto all this knowledge of a place she'd never been. Katya had been there lots and went again the following year. Manon was working then and couldn't go.

Telling Katya about the pieces of glass is a final intimacy Manon refuses to give away. It is a place Manon knows well, where Katya has never been.

In Berlin, Britta never told Katya what it was like for her when Katya returned to Canada. Britta would walk her to the U-bahn station, surrounded by Turkish kebab houses, coffee shops and vegetable vendors, and would allow the public situation to inhibit her affection.

"See ya later, *meine liebe*," she would say, her hands in her pockets. A kiss on Katya's neck and she was gone.

Later, Britta would cry herself to sleep with long, heaving sobs, staying in bed for days. Utta and Marion would show up faithfully and solemnly at Britta's door every morning with chunks of hash and take-out cups of coffee, finally convincing Britta to emerge and sit outdoors at the anarchist café, her bald head unprotected and innocent in the bright morning light.

While Manon and Britta each secretly wonder who it is Katya wants more, neither understands it is the condition of being in between – neither here nor there – that turns Katya on. Katya's identity exists in running for cover, to and from the opposing poles of Britta and Manon.

Katya longs for something more complete, but she's sure she'll never get it. A love that will surround her, a guarantee against abandonment. It is loss she's terrified of, not intimacy like everyone assumes. Having both Manon and Britta, she cuts her losses. Or so it seems.

Britta made love to Katya in a hard, controlled and expert way. Katya watched in wonderment as one of Britta's dildoes went into her for the first time, Britta speaking only in German: tough, dirty words that Katya couldn't understand. She shook with excitement when Britta fucked her in the middle of the night, waking her from sleep and restraining her hands in the network of hooks and straps above the bed. Britta rimmed Katya's anus with a dental dam; showed Katya how to fist her; brought out her whip and stroked Katya's ass; taught Katya how to go beyond the limits of her body's pain.

Katya took some of these things home to Manon and integrated them into their lovemaking in subtle and refined ways. Occasionally, she introduced little vanilla things, like butterfly kisses and tribadism, into her sex with Britta. Sometimes, she forgot what she was introducing to whom.

Once, she woke Britta up in the middle of the night and started fucking her.

"That's nice," said Britta sleepily, teasingly. "Where did you learn this?"

"Oh, I don't know," said Katya, not getting it. "I just like to fuck women in their sleep. They seem to like it."

Britta put her hand on Katya's and made her stop. Then she turned her back and went to sleep.

When Katya was still the new girl in town, Britta treated her like a tourist, taking her to all the standard sites: the Brandenburg Gate, Alexanderplatz and Checkpoint Charlie, where an odd museum stood, an American fantasy of what the Wall represented. Katya and Britta stared for a long time at the huge photographs of East Berliners who had tried to escape over the Wall. There was a series of photos of a man who spent years of evenings after work, digging a tunnel from his backyard into the Free World. His wife would watch him anxiously, bringing his dinners out to the tunnel when he was up late digging. There was another photo series of a woman who packed herself into a suitcase and then had the suitcase packed into the trunk of a car which managed to get across. The suitcase and car were all miraculously in the museum, with a diagram of the woman's folded-up body.

Katya was skeptical, wondering if anyone from the West ever tried to escape to the East. But Britta said quietly, later, as they sat eating *apfelkuchen* in a café across the way: "Those photos are for me about the profoundly human desire for freedom, no matter what the cost. Sometimes this freedom is not as important or as valuable as we had imagined, but we never know this until it's too late."

Berlin in June. There were sidewalk cafés everywhere, even if it was just two chairs and a table on a sidewalk. There were bicycle paths on every street, along the canals and beside outdoor markets exploding with texture and smell: Turkish breads, Indian scarves, bratwurst, vegetables and leather. There was beer that smelled like perfume and beer that tasted like fruit. There were linden trees arching over wide avenues, sending clouds of white into the air. There were old Marlene Dietrich films playing in tiny cinemas that seated 25 people. There were cafés adjoining the cinemas, where the fantasy of the movie continued into discussion: waving arms and important points through cigarette smoke and conversation. And there was the Oranienbar, where women overflowed into

Oranienstrasse, draping themselves over parked cars, necking under streetlamps, leaning into each other's leather jackets.

Katya liked to go to the bar early, before Britta finished her shift.
She would hang out in the crowd on the street, where Britta
couldn't see her. She'd watch Britta through the large windows of
the bar, serving beer in fast-motion, gay men leaning towards her
and trying to whisper in her ear. Katya watched as Britta listened
to the whispered comment and threw back her head and laughed,
maybe touching the man briefly on the shoulder, then moving
away. The more she holds back, the more she is pursued.

By the time Britta got off work, Katya was so turned on she
could hardly stand up. They usually hung out on the street for a
little while, having a cigarette and kissing. One night, Britta
pushed Katya against a car and put her hand down Katya's jeans:
discreetly, quickly. Then, Britta crossed the street and started talking to Dorothea, who had been cruising her for weeks.

Katya acted cool, lit another cigarette and waited. Britta didn't
come back, she walked down the road to the women's disco, and
then to Kreuzberg and the squatter's bar. Britta finally tracked her
down at 3 A.M. She had passion and need in her eyes, which was
exactly what Katya wanted.

Katya has forgotten to send any postcards for a week. Things between her and Britta have been good, ever since their big public
fight outside the bar that night. She phones Manon from Britta's
place, while Britta showers. Katya is stretched out on the bed, her
hand in her crotch.

"Baby, I miss you so much," Katya says. "I think about you all
the time. I'm thinking we shouldn't be apart so much."

Manon's voice is thin and ungenerous on the long-distance line.

"Well, maybe it's you who needs to change something, so we won't be apart so much. Otherwise, we'll be apart much more than you think."

Katya hears the warning, though the connection is bad, warms to it, softens her voice, moves her hand into her own wetness, comforts.

"Baby, I'm sorry. . . . " There is a slight shift in power, discernible even across a transatlantic phone line. It really turns Katya on.

"Baby, I'm gonna make it up to you. I need you to know that I want you so much."

That week, Britta was working twelve-hour days, between the vegetarian café and the bar, so Katya had time to herself. She arranged an interview with Antje, a lesbian in her 80s, who had lived in Berlin during the Weimar period. Katya had intended to arrange this meeting for the longest time, but life with Britta always got in the way.

Antje lived at the end of an U-bahn line, near a forest and a lake. Katya walked through an overgrown park to her tiny cottage. It felt calm here, in this neighbourhood of retired people, tending to rosebushes or walking their dogs. Katya realized she hadn't seen much of Berlin in daylight, she only seemed to go out at night.

Antje greeted her with a hug and Katya felt Antje's cheek against hers, like soft worn leather with the faintest smell of rosewater. Antje sat Katya down in an overstuffed chair and bustled with trays of pastries, cheese, bread and coffee. Katya fiddled with her tape recorder. Her mind wasn't really on the interview; she was wondering where Manon was, what Britta was up to.

Still, the interview went well. Antje seemed happy, delighted even, to be telling her stories, to have someone new in her home, to feed them with pumpernickel bread and beautiful exotic cheeses that Katya had never seen before. They drank coffee out of delicate porcelain cups and saucers decorated with orange blossoms and birds. Afternoon sun moved across the room. Antje talked, slowly and thoughtfully, brushing crumbs out of her lap, savouring each sweet memory, and smiling a crinkly, careful smile when her story turned sad.

"It is like anything else," Antje said. "We had so much, such an abundance of lesbian culture, such a rich night life, and the songs, the poetry, I can't begin to tell you. . . . "

She paused and swallowed, delicately, politely. "And we did not know how much we had, until it was gone, of course.

"They took everything away, but slowly, so very slowly. A bar closes down, you simply go to another, you're young, you want a good time, you don't ask why. Someone disappears, a writer whose work you've read, you're sad, but there are other writers, other books."

Antje was silent for several minutes, trying to reach the precise words for something important she wanted to say. She leaned over to Katya suddenly and held her hand tightly.

"You must fight. You must be clear about what you want and then you must fight for it. Or you will regret it for the rest of your life."

The next day, Katya spent hours gathering coloured pieces of the Wall from the gritty space along the canal, as a souvenir for Manon. She went to the field beside the train tracks, sat among the dried grass and the poppies and wrote Manon a long love letter. The letter was full of memories and full of promises. And Katya made a decision, writing: "Baby, I want to settle down with you."

She mailed the letter right away, so she wouldn't change it. She felt good, clean. She bought flowers for Britta and went to meet her at the bar at midnight, took her home and gave her a massage, held her tired, tight body the whole night through. In the morning, Britta let Katya fuck her unclothed for the first time and came, in a full and vulnerable way.

Katya's letter crossed Manon's letter, somewhere in the middle of the ocean. Perhaps they were both written the same day.

Manon's machine has been on for days, Katya can't get through. None of her friends seem to know where Manon has gone. Britta is working double shifts again and Katya can't get a cheap ticket to Montreal until next week. She's sure she can fix things, if she can only see Manon face-to-face.

Sex with Britta has been transcendant this week. They fucked out in the field and then in the washroom at the vegetarian café. Yesterday, Britta made her wear nipple clamps all evening, under her shirt, and this morning, she let Manon fist her: wide, soft expanse of cunt, surrounding her hand, beating like a heart, insistent and so open.

"*Meine liebe,* this is *good,*" sighed Britta. Afterwards, she looked into Katya's eyes for a long time.

Katya goes to Oranienbar at midnight. Britta is off at one, but Katya wants to hang out. She shares a cigarette with Utta and lets Annetta, the anti-fascist organizer, flirt with her just a little bit. There's a massive march the next day and Katya agrees to leaflet. If she's deported, maybe she'll get home faster.

She turns habitually to check out Britta through the window. Britta is deep in an embrace with the other bartender. They pull back, Katya breathes a sigh of relief, and then they move towards each other again and start to neck passionately. The men at the bar smile, as though they're used to it. One of them applauds. Katya goes back to the apartment. Britta gets home at 6 A.M.

Britta had been expecting anger and tears, maybe wanting them. But Katya has North American therapy words tumbling through her head: *State your needs, stay calm, don't get angry.* She says nothing.

The march begins at dusk, winding through the Turkish neighbourhoods where firebombing by neo-Nazis has been going on recently. Police in riot gear line the streets, a long blue column, light glinting off their clear plastic shields, surreal in the purple evening light. There are thousands of people, and all the dykes from the bars, the cafés and the neighbourhood are marching together, a band of leather jackets and spiked hair. Antje walks arm-in-arm with her partner Gerda. They wave eagerly at Katya. There are Turkish Maoists and American ex-patriots and Afro-German women and mothers with children who Katya has seen at the Hammam Baths and leftists and sad-looking older people who remember what it was like before.

The march lasts for hours, twisting through narrow streets. Some Maoists burn a German flag on the sidewalk and the flames cast an oddly beautiful glow in the store windows. At one point, Katya turns to Britta and says: "I love you. I'll stay, if you want me to."

Britta laughs, then gets serious, takes her aside into an alleyway and kisses her deep.

"Darlin', I gotta tell you. I'm gonna be seein' someone else now. It's a whole different thing I'm tryin'. It's really important to me. You can come visit when you want. But don't say this kinda thing anymore."

They return to the march. Some anti-fascist skinheads are

breaking windows which splinter, white and sparkling, into the air. Katya keeps walking with Britta until she sees a phone booth, glowing yellow in the darkness. She runs to it, pulls out her Bell calling card, starts dialling. It's 4 A.M. in Montreal. Like a miracle, she gets through, she's crying, saying love words, saying she'll be home soon, sooner than expected. Manon agrees to meet her, but there is a *silence*, a wall of something that wasn't there before. Katya stays in the phone booth long after the line's gone dead, watching the march pass by, blurry and dreamlike through her tears.

II

CONNECTING FLIGHT

Tempting Fire

And that was the end of our friendship for a long time,
this quarrel in which we did not know how to negoti-
ate power when it broke into the love between us. . . .
MINNIE BRUCE PRATT, The Friends of My Secret Self

"So. Do you have a lover?" asks Lisa, whose house this is.

"Well, yes. Kind of. We have one of those loose-knit, open relation-ships," says Ruta, the woman who is in town for a few days. "And you?"

"No. Not for a while. It's a time for me to be alone." Lisa sighs, goes to the fridge, gets two beers.

"Do you, ah, ever have affairs?" asks Ruta suddenly, trying to keep her voice neutral, not succeeding.

The fridge door slams shut.

"Oh yeah. We don't usually end up on speaking terms, though."

"Oh well. C'est la vie, I guess."

"Yeah."

"Yeah."

Cecily and Ruta are meeting for breakfast at the Varsity, their favourite greasyspoon on Bloor Street West. It's the only time Cecily, who is booked every minute this week, can spare. Ruta, artist-on-a-grant, sighs, complies.

Cecily and Ruta: heads tilting towards each other, eyes swerving, voices lowering periodically. Silence as the waitress refills the coffee, then leaning forward again, whispering furiously. They could be arranging a drug deal or a coup.

They are discussing their love lives. ("And *then*," whispers Cecily, "just as we were about to enter the subway, she pushed me against a wall and said: 'I want to kiss you, *now*.' Unfortunately, I immediately got paralysis.")

They are both fervently practising non-monogamy, as though it had recently been invented by them. Ruta and Cecily have been best friends for ten years. They are each other's continuity: their lives a frantic sequence of political involvements and ruptures; sexual adventures and setbacks; evictions, roommate crises and landlord problems. Not to mention Ruta's cycle of unemployment and grants, and Cecily's string of social services burnout jobs.

Ruta is back from a trip. She manages to fly around the country on artist gigs, while living just below the poverty line. She has had a miniature affair in Victoria, is pale, distraught.

"Cec, it was so . . . awkward. We had this absolutely primal connection and then she refused to sleep with me. I mean, we did, finally. . . . "

"You did finally what? *Sleep?*" Cecily's eyes widen. Her hand, carrying toast to her mouth, freezes in mid-air.

"No . . . we . . . ah, fucked. I mean, it took a while, it was 3 A.M., but yeah, we had sex. . . . "

The toast drops dramatically from Cecily's hand. She sighs with relief.

" . . . but she wouldn't let me stay the night. And the next day she drives me to the airport, cool as can be, as though nothing's happened between us."

Cecily shovels poached eggs and homefries into her mouth, synthesizes, sympathizes.

"The girl is obviously dealing with some kind of repression. You forget, Ruthie, not everyone is as *out* as we are. Who knows *what* they're talking about in Victoria. She's probably *anti-porn!* Did you ask her?"

"No. It never came up." Ruta hangs her head.

Cecily wipes her mouth with her napkin, takes Ruta's hand in hers, holding it tightly. Like Ruta, she is intensely passionate about everything, no matter how small. Cecily came out five years ago, Ruta a year after that. Both were shocked to discover a no-man's zone devoid of rules or ethics; uncharted desert between the outposts of sex and love, and no indication of where the borders, if any, existed.

"Ruthie honey, it's *normal* for you to be a little, tiny bit sad. Just don't send Lisa any love letters, okay, not just yet." Ruta wants to be normal. The daughter of refugees, a history of invasions and hard labour camps a mere generation behind her, she wants to be, well . . . normal.

She worries she's too intense, too serious, too guilt-ridden. What's more, she's afraid she'll never meet a single socialist-feminist dyke who could match her own, or Cecily's, stamina. To eye one another at coalition meetings. To lie in bed with someone and ruthlessly analyze the breakdown of Soviet communism. To eat breakfast together and discuss lesbian sexuality in the context of post-modernist theories of representation.

She's way too obsessive and it shows. Obsessive about anyone she's attracted to, anything she's interested in. Sometimes she catches an image of herself in a mirror or a store window: eyes narrowed behind horn-rimmed glasses, full Slavic lips in a pout, body bent forward at a hurried tilt, a bad-hair day, most days. *But your lips are sexy,* said Cecily, once. Who but Cecily could handle Ruta's ancestral legacy of melancholy and romanticism, not to mention her constant need to analyze every single event of the day?

For Cecily, daughter of alcoholics and manic-depressives, intensity is a way of life, a world view, an absolute necessity. She lives her life at full emotional capacity, invisible faultlines quavering just below the surface. But to Ruta, Cecily is beautiful in her intensity and Cecily is everything Ruta is not: a perfect Gap look; shiny, straight black hair she constantly runs her fingers through, as though shaking away some demon; classic, trim Anglo nose; a cigarette always in her graceful hand.

Cecily and Ruta, holding hands in the crowded greasyspoon, looking for all the world like illicit lovers. Content to be each other's mirror, refracting light, creating heat, tempting fire.

Ruta and Lisa sit quietly in the fading winter light. Ruta takes small, nervous sips from her Kokanee beer and sneaks glimpses of the harbour, barely visible through the window. The view helps her deal with the sexual tension rising like fog in the kitchen. Lisa's two dogs, Gertrude and Alice, watch Ruta closely. Lisa clears her throat. Ruta swallows. Gertrude growls. A foghorn moans in the distance.

"It's been really nice getting to know you," ventures Ruta, finally.

Lisa has been peeling the label off her beer bottle. She looks up, startled, wary.

"Yeah. Same here."

"And well, the thing is, I find you incredibly attractive." The dogs sit up. Lisa blinks. Ruta's stomach contracts.

"Oh. Well. Thank you. That's flattering."

Alice yawns.
Oh no.

Cecily and Ruta are Christmas shopping. Or rather Ruta, who doesn't have any extra cash this year, is helping Cecily shop. Christmas for Cecily is like a monsoon or a blizzard: a regular natural disaster for which she is always, chronically, unprepared. Loaded with shopping bags full of feminist children's books and teenage Ninja products, they touch down at a vegetarian restaurant on Queen Street West where the food, they both agree, smells oddly, faintly, of meat. But Cecily has environmental allergies; at least here she can order the tofu casserole. Ruta sighs, complies, manages to locate something vaguely lethal on the menu, orders coffee and deep-fried tempeh with ketchup on the side.

"Ruth, I just don't know how I'm gonna handle Christmas this year. My mother gets released from the psych ward December 23rd. My father says he's going on the wagon – just like that, cold turkey, pardon the pun – on December 24th. They'll probably *kill* each other by Christmas day. And my sister's coming in from Pickering with her four kids. Her husband's just left her, turns out he's been slapping her around for years, she's on Valium. . . . "

Ruta takes a deep breath.

"Cec, why go?"

"What do you mean? You don't understand, I have to. . . . "

"No, look, why not skip it this year. Give them some excuse, tell them you have a highly contagious virus, tell them you're a lesbian, anything. Spend Christmas with me and Carmen, we're having a bunch of dyke Christmas orphans over, it'll be great, lots of food, old movies, we'll make a special tofu turkey just for you."

"*You don't understand.* They're *expecting* me, my mother phones me twice a day, asking if I'm sure I'm coming home. . . . "

"I know, sweetie, I know. But it's the same every year. She phones you and phones you, you go, you have a rotten time, you're depressed for a month afterwards, so is she. I mean, most of us come from dysfunctional families; at some point we have to figure out ways to. . . . "

"You're trivializing my experience!" Cecily pushes her plate of food away. "Your family isn't at *all* like mine. You don't know what it's like having your mother in a psych ward, you have no idea what it's like dealing with an alcoholic father."

Ruta looks around nervously, then leans toward Cecily, touching her arm gingerly.

"Look hon, I'm sorry, I didn't mean to offend you, I was only trying to help. I do know a little bit what it's like cuz you've told me and I just hate to see you go through this year after year."

"You have *no right* to make assumptions about how I should handle this! You have *no right* telling me what to do!

Ruta has spent her entire life carefully avoiding public scenes like this one. She sits, open-mouthed, staring, as Cecily continues to shout at her. An image of herself as a little girl flashes in her mind and disappears. She doesn't leave.

Several days later, Cecily phones Ruta, tearful and apologetic. She had terrible PMS, her allergies were acting up, the Christmas thing was getting to her, she thinks she was projecting her childhood anger onto Ruta, she's *really really* sorry. Ruta murmurs understandingly: it's okay, it's okay, it's a difficult time of year.

Five minutes pass in Lisa's kitchen, marked by the clicking of digital clock numbers over the stove. The dogs move closer to Lisa, who puts her beer down and places her hands flat on the table, as though about to close a deal.

"So what are you trying to say?" she asks in a flat voice, though her blue eyes flash.

Ruta attempts ambiguity and nonchalance.

"You wanna . . . er . . . hang out? Tonight, that is," she shrugs.

"Hang out. You mean, have sex."

"Well, yeah. That's it. . . . " Ruta grins, relieved.

"And you're leaving tomorrow."

Ruta nods. Alice wags her tail. Lisa mulls this over, chin in hand.

"Well now, I just don't know." She smiles and then doesn't.

Ruta realizes there is no going back now. She dives into a clear pool of honesty, explaining how she'd like to hold Lisa's long, lean body, explore her broad shoulders, kiss her serious intent face, gaze into her pale blue eyes. Lisa watches Ruta closely as she talks. Ruta can feel herself getting wetter and wetter. Shadows grow in the kitchen, which seems to have become smaller, warmer.

Ruta is doing January Christmas in Winnipeg with her family. Spent the last of her Canada Council grant on presents and a plane ticket, hasn't been there in three years, is sick with worry.

"It'll be *great*," says Cecily, negotiating the expressway at rush hour, rushing Ruta to the airport on time. Ruta is in the backseat trying to zip up her suitcase, socks and lesbian novels straining at the seams. "Ruth, you're *much* more confident than you used to be."

Ruta lets go of the zipper. *After Dolores* and *Macho Sluts* fall out.

"Oh, so I was a nerd before?"

"You were less . . . happy before. You hadn't come out, you hadn't met Carmen, you hadn't started being the gay, rakish gal you are now. Now you're more . . . you."

"Cecily, enough."

"Anyways, it'll be *fine*. You got those books I lent you?"

"Yeah, yeah. . . . "

"Bury yourself in Sarah Schulman, call me every night if you need to. Well, call Carmen too. Remember to *breathe* when you get tense, don't argue with your mother, bring me back some cabbage rolls, you'll be fine."

"You been reading Louise Hay or what?"

"Nope. But you know what?"

"What?"

"I have a date on Friday night with Rhonda Levitin."

"Oh, Cec."

While Ruta checks her luggage, Cecily runs to the gift shop, fills a bag with Smarties, Bazooka gum and M&M's, fishes the December issue of *On Our Backs* from her knapsack and throws that in, runs back and hands the bag to Ruta who immediately bursts into tears.

Ruta feels fear tightening the inside of her throat. She can't even explain it to Cecily and nothing feels complete until it is told to Cecily.

"Cec, I'm just so fuckin' nerved out."

"I know, Ruthie, I know." Cecily doesn't know, feels unequal to the task of giving advice. To Cecily, Ruta's bulky Eastern European family is the stuff of CBC ethnic drama: adorable, sweet, totally unreal.

"I love you Ruthie"

"I love you too"

They embrace, wrapped in each other for several minutes, oblivious to the solemn stares of winter tourists filing out of customs in Gore-Tex parkas and sombreros.

Ruta spends a week in Winnipeg. The nightmares begin as soon as she comes home.

" . . . so I've been on my own for the past two years," Lisa is saying. "I'm trying not to jump into anything. I've got a lot of stuff I'm dealing with."

"Oh, god, am I ever embarrassed, I totally misread the situation, I'm really. . . . "

"You haven't misread anything," says Lisa slowly, evenly. She gets up from her chair and puts her empty beer bottle away. She stands in front of the window for a moment, looking outside and flexing her shoulders, stretching her arms. Ruta admires Lisa's back, muscular and tender beneath a thin white T-shirt. The silence in the room is poignant, and full.

Lisa moves to where Ruta is sitting, puts her hands on Ruta's shoulders, rubs the base of her neck.

"I'd love to sleep with you," Lisa whispers. Ruta emits a tiny sigh. Gertrude wakes from a dream and barks, suddenly.

"But I can't. I just . . . can't. Please don't take it personally. Could I just give you a massage instead?"

It's February. Ruta is napping on her couch by the window, trying to out-sleep a low-level virus that has hung on since January. She is able to sleep only in the daytime, afternoon sunlight like gentle touch on her body. Nights are ragged with images, tossing and pacing, and cup after cup of Sleepytime tea.

She's missed the last Canada Council deadline. "That's okay," Cecily counselled over the phone, "you'll just apply for the next one."

But Ruta is attuned to grant deadlines as though they are the cycles of the moon, her creativity long ago corrupted by the biannual promise of cash. She can't believe she let this one slip by, she needs the money to finish her project, to get through the year.

Carmen has just left. There's chicken soup on the stove, fresh blood-red tulips in a vase, a ten-pound self-help book on the table. Ruta closes her eyes, sees an image of her Uncle Yurij, his shirt unbuttoned. Opens her eyes quickly, closes them, sees Cecily dancing in the bar, graceful, beautiful, her black hair pulled back, her eyes on fire. Opens and closes her eyes again: embroidered pillows, an icon on the wall.

It's Cecily, not Carmen, not anyone else, that Ruta wants here now. Cecily would know what to say or do. *Cecily.* Is not there.

"Sweetie, I know it's hard for you right now. I wish I could be there for you but things have been so frantic. Mom's in the psych ward again and Dad isn't handling it very well. We're really busy at work and I'm painting my apartment and meanwhile, the Coalition of Rape Crisis Centres has elected *me* chairperson. On top of all that, Rhonda's going *nuts* over her thesis. . . . "

Rhonda?

"Yeah, Rhonda Levitin, remember? It all happened pretty fast. It's scary, I haven't been this close to someone for a while. I mean it's great, too, the sex is great, her politics are great. Honey, it'll cut into our time but I need for you to be happy for me, I really do. Ruth . . . Ruthie, are you still there?"

Nightmares. Strange memories. Fear, grief, panic, in the super-market, in the middle of the day.

"What are you doing to take care of yourself? Have you been seeing your therapist? Are you eating properly? You know, there's a book you might want to look at, it's called *Courage My Love* or something."

Embroidered pillows on the bed: red, orange, yellow, green. An icon at the foot of the bed, a Byzantine Jesus, embroidered towel draped around it.

"Ruta, I'm feeling some anger from you and I can't handle it, I really can't, you're going to have to. . . . "

Ruta hangs up, as though in a trance.

Cecily doesn't process the phone call for a long time, because there isn't time. Her mom gets worse. Cecily goes to the hospital twice a day, sits in a blank peach-coloured room and holds her hand. She tries to ask questions of the doctors, who are surly and suspicious. She tries to get her mother to eat the bizarre hospital food: vegetables in lime aspic and hamburgers substantial as hockey pucks. Rhonda drives Cecily to the hospital when she can but Cecily starts getting mad at Rhonda, just because she's *there*: why is Rhonda so silent, why was Rhonda late? Rhonda patiently waits for these moods to pass. Cecily doesn't want patience, she wants engagement, wants a fight like Ruta would give her.

But Ruta is so watery now, so plaintive and Cecily is afraid. No one is there with her, in the inner chamber of her terror. No one. But her.

Ruta sleeps through February. By March, she's woken up, does a major laundry, makes love with Carmen for the first time in three months, a halting, almost childlike lovemaking, half pleasure and half pain.

She skips International Women's Day for fear she'll run into Cecily. They've stopped talking, she hardly knows why.

Carmen goes on the march with her battered women's shelter collective and Ruta spends the day at the Cineplex. Twenty-eight dollars, four films, she sits in dark rooms and feels the coloured images flicker warm over her eyes. Halfway through *Dances with*

Wolves she realizes she hardly knew where Cecily ended and Ruta began. She can't sort out the images or the pain.

Embroidery, chenille bedspread, Cecily's black leather jacket, her smell of soap and musk oil, the whiskey on her uncle's breath at Christmas time.

She can't figure out who's the abuser, who's the victim, who set up whom.

"My heart splits in two. I feel my skin closing up, tight as can be. . . .

"I try to allow the touch of another woman, breathe in her smell, let it enter my skin. She tells me how she'd like to make love to me but my body feels hard and numb. . . .

"The more I remember about the incest, the more alone I feel. I try to talk to my friends but I feel their eyes glaze over with disbelief. I try to be close to this woman but I hear my body say, 'no.' . . .

"I feel like everything is changing, like nothing will ever be the same again. . . . "

Ruta holds Lisa's story in her hand. She found it unexpectedly in a women's paper at the bookstore, flipping casually through the pages as she stood at the magazine rack. Bought it, took it home, reads it over and over again.

Cecily is strolling along Bloor, moving slowly the way you do when the air gets soft after a long winter. She walks with her jacket open, her face up, feeling the sun. She sees Ruta coming out of Bloor Supersave – Ruta used to call it Bloor Superspend – two blocks away. The streets are crowded but she'd recognize Ruta's leather jacket and her long, quick stride anywhere. A lost coin, glinting in the sun.

Cecily opens her mouth. Her throat aches. It's too far to shout Ruta's name. Cecily starts to walk faster. A crowd of anarchist teenagers is hanging out on the sidewalk, playing music, and she has to go around them. She looks again. Ruta has disappeared.

Maybe she imagined her. Lately she's been seeing Ruta everywhere, tenses her body to either say hello or look away, then realizes it's someone else. Ruta has called twice, leaving messages on Cecily's phone machine in the daytime, when she knows Cecily is not at home. Cecily has not returned her calls. Once, they ran into each other at a gallery opening, awkwardly making conversation in the crowd: Ruta flushed and stammering, Cecily hating to see her that way, wanting to help, but repelled by so much need. She hardly recognizes Ruta when she's like that, feels betrayed somehow. She wants the witty banter, the empathy, the strength, that used to flow like a warm steady current between them. At night, she dreams it's Ruta in her mother's hospital bed, looking up at her, crying, desperate, begging her please to stay.

Cecily dreams constantly of hands pulling at her, grabbing her clothes, her hair, begging for attention and love, as though she were a mother with too many children. But in the dream, she is only five years old.

She misses Ruta deeply, a hole in her heart that no one else can fill.

A clear Friday night in May and Ruta wanders along Dundas Street West, a handful of stars in the sky, a patient moon peering through the smog. A night to herself.

A night to myself, Ruta says to herself, trying hard to appreciate it. She thinks of her mother, no nights to herself for 20 years. She thinks of when she was busier, how she often said she longed for nights like this.

A night to herself. She is fortunate, she thinks.

A week of meetings and grant applications had left her too pre-occupied to plan for the weekend. She wasn't used to planning weekends anyway, there had always been Cecily or Carmen. Recently, she added a personal section to her to-do list. 'Clean out closet' and 'phone Jo-Ann' have been carried over from week to week since April. Other regular entries included: 'buy flowers' . . . 'phone YW re: membership' . . . 'phone rape crisis centre re: incest support group.' Perhaps, muses Ruta as she rounds the corner to the liquor store, she should have added 'plan Friday night' to the list.

She had finally phoned Jo-Ann, waiting until Thursday, calling her at work on the pretext of getting a mailing list for the women artists' conference Ruta was organizing. *By-the-way-do-you-feel-like-going-for-a-beer-or-a-movie-sometime-maybe-tomorrow,* Ruta blurted at the end of the conversation. Jo-Ann said yes. By the time she hung up the phone, Ruta's shirt was soaked in sweat. She picked up the receiver again, dialled three numbers, then realized what she was doing. She had forgotten. She and Cecily weren't speaking anymore. She hardly remembered why.

The next morning, Jo-Ann left a message on Ruta's machine, cancelling their date. She should have checked her almanac, she had something else on that night, it had totally slipped her mind, she's real busy these days, she'd try to call again sometime. Soon.

So it is that Ruta wanders, comforting herself with rationaliza-tions. Jo-Ann is blonde, Anglo, not her type. Ruta's mother would not even know how to say such a name, would slur the *J* and soften the *A*. Jo-Ann is too femmy, too liberal, too tall.

Too tall? Ruta is herself five feet, seven inches. It was simply not meant to be. She laughs as she enters the liquor store, splurges on a bottle of white Chardonnay and then decides to keep walking instead of going home to her bathtub. It's unseasonably warm, even for May. The night seems full of electric currents and a blue neon-glow of possibility.

Ruta walks for a long time, past the Portuguese fish stores, as lively and packed with people as the women's bar on a Saturday night. She looks into the windows of renovated homes around Bellwoods Park and, politically incorrectly, sighs at the pleasure of sandblasted brick and restored stained glass. She passes young yuppie couples walking along College, licking his and hers cones of *gelato* from the Bar Italia, and Italian families digging into silver bowls of *tartufo* at the Sicilian Ice Cream Parlour. She hears three older women arguing in Ukrainian about the Blue Jays game as they wait for the College streetcar. She sees two dykes with matching haircuts huddled over espresso at the Café Diplomatico, their knees barely touching.

When she gets to Bathurst, however, she can hardly see anything. The streetlights are off, the streetcars aren't running. There's been a blackout. Too many people had turned on their air-conditioners, due to the May heatwave.

For a few hours, the streets become a pre-industrial time warp. Except for the corner stores, the shops on Bloor are closed for fear of looting, so Ruta passes pizza cooks and stereo salesmen lounging and chatting with each other on the street, sharing cigarettes. She goes into a mom-and-pop store lit with candles, children hovering around them like excited moths. Back on the sidewalk, she bumps into high-rise tenants, bored because the Jays TV game has been interrupted. They are throwing impromptu block parties in front of their buildings, passing around cartons of ice cream rescued from their melting freezers. Some have radios and are calling out the baseball scores as a community service. At the movie complex at Yonge and Bloor, crowds of people are sitting on the front steps. They had to leave halfway through so they're talking together and nervously imagining how the film might have ended.

Energized by all this unexpected activity, Ruta keeps walking all the way to the women's bar on Parliament. She wants to check out how the lesbian nation is coping with the blackout. At the Rose Café, she is surrounded by women spilling into the street. Some have flashlights. There's a woman with bobbed red hair who looks a bit like Nancy Drew. Inside the bar, there are candles everywhere and a bartender carries a camping lantern. It's quiet except for the hum of women's voices.

Ruta buys a warm beer for half price and leans against the bar. The woman who looks like Nancy Drew comes in and asks her for a cigarette. Ruta doesn't smoke but she holds the flashlight as Nancy Drew takes one from the bartender. All around her, women are talking about the warm weather and the Jays game and the upcoming choice rally. They argue about the federal deficit and whether it's okay to like s/m and what proof there is that Dolly Parton's a dyke. Their faces are beautiful, soft and gold in the reflected light of candles and camping lanterns.

Nancy Drew and Ruta talk. They don't exchange names but they tell each other coming-out stories and funny date-gone-wrong stories and ex-lover-from-hell stories. Because the clocks have broken down, no one notices it's 3 A.M. and the bar is still open. At 4 A.M., the owner passes around warm orange juice, on the house. At 5 A.M., the streetlights come on and the sun begins to rise. Everybody moves to leave, slowly, regretfully. Nancy Drew and Ruta find themselves on the sidewalk, just as the birds start to sing. A mauve light fills the sky. Ruta knows what's coming next but she isn't sure what she'll say.

Nancy Drew turns off her flashlight and says, in a probing, girl-detective kind of way: "So, I was wondering. Do you have a lover?"

"No," says Ruta. She pauses and hears herself say: "It's a time for me to be alone."

She kisses Nancy Drew affably, on both cheeks, as though they are in Paris or Montreal. Then she catches the College streetcar home.

Familia

SHE'S CRAWLING OUT of a slippery tunnel of sleep, trying to haul her dream with her like an elusive fish, light and memory catching on all its scales. The dream is a 60s home movie about her family, flickering through a desert in a shiny red car, trying to get to Ukraine by a roundabout route, her father pulls out a map and suddenly it's a documentary, an old National Film Board kind with a lot of narration, only it's Brian's voice, her upstairs neighbour and it's morning. . . .

"Hey, Ruth, *lève-toi*, I've got your opera tapes for you." For some reason she has her message machine turned up. Brian's melodious fag voice drawls through the apartment.

What's going on? The fish falls out of her hands.

Then Brian is at the door, a huge grin on his face, with an armful of Mozart arias: Jessye Norman, Maria Callas and a compilation tape he made, called Leave it to Diva. As well as the latest issue of *Village Voice* and a copy of *Toronto Life*.

"I can't stay, I'm meeting Yves for breakfast, you mentioned something about wanting to listen to opera, so here's a sampling of my favourites, plus Jody Foster's been outed, it's in the *Voice,* and I thought you might enjoy this mag to quell your incipient home-sickness. . . . No, I can't have coffee, Yves hates it when I'm late, he's so . . . *exigeant!*" Brian leaves in a flurry of giggles, off to his 24-year-old lover, his carefully arranged mid-50s' pleasure and distraction.

It's true, she did say something about opera days ago. She didn't say she was homesick but in fact she is, though she'd be at a loss to say where home is. Ruta puts someone named Marilyn Horne into the tape deck – *"Mon coeur s'ouvre à ta voix"* – grinds beans for coffee, sits in the rocking chair facing Mount Royal, mauve in the spring morning light. Song fills the silent space of her apartment where she lives, alone, in her thirty-third year.

You're travelling through a desert, meeting to meeting to meeting, swaying inside various streetcars, men rub up against you, you pull away, nausea in your throat, acid in your stomach, you're thirsty, for what you don't exactly know, and your mama always said: "If you don't know what you want, it means you don't want," but maybe, just this once, your mama is wrong and you are on your own.

Community is an unattainable mirage on the horizon, but sweet moments of solidarity are the oases. You're sitting at a greasyspoon on Bloor after an International Women's Day Coalition meeting. Your proposal on poverty issues was soundly quashed, there are 20,000 homeless in this city, so here you are now drinking beer with your anti-poverty collective. Some other women from the meeting join you, you say how discouraged you feel and a Black woman who years ago sat on the opposite side of a room and called you on your racism is saying: "We have to organize for the long-term, we are in this strug-gle for our lives," and it's only later that you realize the courage it took for her to say 'we.'

In between there are days, weeks when you travel non-stop, the land beneath your feet constantly shifting, you long to find your own safe space, your people, your piece of land.

"But darlin', I *want* to meet your family, I want to know where you're from. . . . "

Ruta is going to chill, still Winnipeg for Ukrainian Christmas in January. It's only November but already they are negotiating the season, she and Eleanor, celebrations balanced on the razor edge of expectation and anticipated pain.

It is two years before they will break up and months before the arguments begin. They are in the stage of new knowledge, each a re-written text endlessly fascinating to the other, and Eleanor is saying: "I want to know the family of the woman I love."

Ruta usually keeps lovers and family on separate planets but this time she gets talked into it, seduced by the promise of something she has never known: a table with her father, mother, brothers and lover around it, she with them, sharing a meal.

They arrange the most treacherous of plans. They will stay at Oksana's place – Ruta's childhood friend – in Winnipeg. Ruta will do Ukrainian Christmas Eve on her own with the family. Eleanor will join them at brunch the next day, officially billed as Ruta's roommate.

All goes according to plan. Brunch is dim sum and Eleanor establishes rapport with Ruta's father immediately because she, unlike anyone else at the table, actually listens to his analysis of the Bolshevik invasion. Mama is unusually agitated, saying loudly: "Where are those dumplings I ordered, I can't believe how slow these Chinese waitresses are. . . . " Eleanor's political reflexes are lightning-quick from fifteen years of demos and meetings. She spins around in her chair and says to Ruta's mother: "She's awfully busy, it's got nothing to do with her being Chinese except that she's probably being paid less than minimum wage." Mama turns silent, the whole table gets rigor mortis, Ruta's father peers suspiciously at them both. When they leave, Mama says: "Let Ruta leave the tip, she can make up for those waitresses being underpaid."

Later, during the flight home, Eleanor blurts suddenly: "Why didn't you say anything, why didn't you support me?" Ruta says nothing. It's impossible to explain. And a small, almost invisible crack appears in the unbroken surface of their love.

You dream you're travelling between two countries, you're at the train station and you can't get on the train, it's going too fast or the platform falls away, but in the dream your Baba has given you bread to eat, her special Easter bread rich with egg yolk, raisins and the leavening of her hands kneading the dough for hours. The bread is all you have, you eat it all through the dream and finally, unlike in other dreams, you manage to get on that train.

There is no avoiding this reunion. Aunt Ruta is on the phone from Winnipeg. She has finally been allowed to leave her tiny village just outside Lviv and is doing a tour of all her Canadian relatives. She will be in Toronto tomorrow night. She is visiting a childhood friend in Scarborough and she expects to see Ruta – her niece, her namesake – that very weekend. Ruta immediately imagines an interrogation, held captive with Ukrainian food while she explains why she's still not married. She's evasive, non-committal, she says she's working long hours this week and she's not sure she'll have time. Aunt Ruta did not spend her youth in the para-military

Ukrainian nationalist underground for nothing. She is determined that Ruta, her niece, will pay homage.

"You, you're my namesake," she is saying in Ukrainian over the
phone. "I keep your photo on my bureau at home. You look so
much like your poor deceased grandmother once did, with your
long hair and your blue eyes, may she rest in peace, what horrors,
what suffering your Baba knew."

Ruta doesn't know what horrors Aunt Ruta is talking about and
her own hair is now spiky-short and streaked with orange. She
phones Oksana immediately.

Oksana is merciless in her analysis.

"Well, thanks to the breakdown of Soviet communism they're
coming here in droves, everybody's fifth cousin from the village,
they want VCRs and blue jeans and politically, *well* . . . you should
hear them talk about the Jews."

Ruta refers to her history book and there it is: anti-Semitism,
the pogroms. And this, too: the Nazi occupation, her uncle killed,
her father in a concentration camp and, of course, the famine, four
million starved to death by Stalin.

She phones Eleanor, who is pragmatic, as usual.

"Look, you don't have to go, you gotta stop trying to always
please your family."

Ruta agrees but doesn't say that the visit with Aunt Ruta exists
somewhere between obligation and desire. It is, finally, about
wanting to hear a story you're in, the kind where, if this event or
that invasion had or hadn't occurred, you would not have been
born. An unrecorded story which Ruta must search for in strange
places. Sometimes she thinks Eleanor wants to only hear about
Easter eggs and funny anecdotes about her Baba, and won't see the
parts of her history that live in the aching heart of difference, in the
places where their bodies and pasts do not connect. Ruta decides,

after the phone call, to go, and Eleanor, inexplicably, is miffed.

Two days later, Ruta makes the long, mysterious streetcar trip to the east end of Toronto, then takes an expensive cab ride to the depths of Scarberia. Her destination is a seedy high-rise, Ukrainian names on half the buzzers. *What a strange exile,* thinks Ruta, what a dubious victory over the Polish landlords and the Russian imperialists. She passes through a lobby whose dust and furniture are vintage 40s and boards an elevator that reluctantly creaks its way to the fifteenth floor.

But when she enters the apartment, there are familiar smells and sights: pickled herring, rye bread, steaming *perishky* coming out of the oven, poppyseed roll on the formica counter and torte: seven layers, she counts them. Aunt Ruta is kissing her three times, hugging her with bony tenacity. Her friends, Petro and Marika Michalchuk, stand behind her, grinning excitedly. Petro, in double-breasted suit and 70s wide tie, takes her jacket.

"Dat's real leather, eh," he says approvingly, in English, to show he's hip, and then goes to get her some *horivka,* a scotch and soda whose stiffness she appreciates fully only the next morning. She realizes, too late, that this is an Occasion, she should have worn a dress or at least a better pair of pants, bright lipsticked smiles flash up at her, she is a giant, towering above these two old ladies in the final decade of their lives. They are giggling like schoolgirls.

"Marika, she was my best friend, but she was always stealing boys from me, didn't you Marichka, *nu!*" Aunt Ruta nudges her comrade, who chortles uproariously, a dry husky laugh rising from ancient lungs that quickly turns into gasping and then coughing. Petro hastily pours her a vodka, she downs it, lands in an armchair and is fine.

Aunt Ruta wastes no time. She has done her research.

"*Nu,* Rutechko, tell me about this feminism of yours." She leans close. Ruta can see the white down on her lip, the gold teeth, the liver spots freckling her parchment skin.

Ruta opens her mouth. Nothing comes out. As if to help, Petro pads silently to her chair and refills her glass.

"Heh, feminism, you think that's something new," Marika butts in. "We had feminists in our time in Ukraine. They were poets and writers, they never married, they were *revered* and now I read in the newspapers about you young women, starting over again and I feel sorry for you. I really do."

Ruta closes her mouth. Aunt Ruta nods her head, satisfied. She leans forward again. This time, there is a touch of craftiness to her manner. She puts her hand on Ruta's knee.

"I hear you went to Nicaragua."

Ruta is impressed by such investigative skill. Nicaragua is some-how easier to describe than feminism. She describes the coffee co-operative she worked on, the hills and the tropical birds, the sound of tortillas being slapped from hand to hand at four in the morn-ing. She tells stories about the campesinas she met, their long dou-ble day, picking coffee, then doing laundry by hand in the river, then dinner, then dragging their drunken husbands home from the cantina.

To Aunt Ruta, her stories sound more familiar than strange. "So what's the difference?" Aunt Ruta says. "Why fight for them and not for your own people?"

Half-time. Petro moves in with more beverages. Marika proffers hot *perishky* succulent with spicy cabbage stuffing, kolbassa, cu-cumbers with garlic, dill, sour cream. Ruta chews and smiles as the two old women describe a 55-year-old highschool prank in spec-tacular detail. They ply her with photographs: there are several of them arm-in-arm or back-to-back, lounging romantically against a blossoming linden tree, hands intertwined, circa 1930.

Now it is Ruta's turn to lean forward towards her aunt, to swallow hard and say: "Aunt, what happened during the war . . . the Jews. . . . "

Her aunt waves her hand, swallows some food.

"The Jews, they were put in camps . . . you don't know, your father, he was in a camp too."

"But our people, the ones that weren't taken away . . . did they say *nothing* about what was happening to the Jews?"

Returning from the kitchen, Marika gasps, shakes her head.

"Our land was taken away from *beneath our feet*," she interjects. "One invasion after another, we couldn't even call ourselves Ukrainian anymore. Then when we came here it just continued, they called us everything but what we were . . . Ruthenians, Austrians, Galicians . . . *bohunks.* Do you have any idea what it is like to have your *soul* taken away?"

There is silence. Marika stands in the middle of the room. Her hand is on her heart, she is breathing rapidly. Everyone looks at Ruta across an impossible barrier of lost history and memory. Even Petro abandons her, ignores her empty glass.

"We didn't know about the Jews, we were too busy being invaded or imprisoned." Marika turns around heavily, goes to slice the torte and make the coffee.

But Ruta has done her research too and faces her aunt again.

"My Uncle Lubomyr, your brother. He was in the German army, I know this, my father once showed me his registration card. I know that he died soon after he signed up, *but why was he there?*"

Aunt Ruta accepts coffee from Marika, blows on it, sighs.

"Lubko, he was very young. He was, let me see, he was fifteen. The Germans came one week to our village, the Bolsheviks the next. All the young men were ordered to sign up, it was complete chance who got them first. We begged Lubko to go underground with us, but he believed them, they promised good food, new clothes, and education, things we never had.

"Certainly there was anti-Semitism in our village. In this we did not participate but it is possible to say that, by doing nothing, we condoned it. Do you think I am proud of this? And perhaps in this way we also hurt ourselves. We lost Lubomyr, we almost lost your father. I did not see him again for 40 years. At that time we did not yet know about the camps."

Ruta is heady with all this honesty and perhaps just slightly drunk. Her voice rises, she is suddenly a child who wants something.

"But that was 1938 when he died. Where were you when they were killing Jews in the camps?"

Aunt Ruta laughs bitterly.

"I was safe. I was in Siberia. That is where they sent me. I was 32 when the Russians let me go back to Ukraine. I was your age and I had already spent ten years in prison. *And for what?*" She covers her eyes with her hands.

Une nuit blanche. *You're awake in the middle of the night, you have no dreams. Sharp stones tumble inside your head. Your bed is an island in the middle of a vast grey ocean, you know you have friends and family and that your phone machine twinkles with messages of good will, but on a night like this, death exists right beside life, ghosts lurk in the corners of the ceiling and the days are shorter than they've ever been.*

Such a plate Greg places before her: pink salmon glistening with butter and silver rind; vegetables tossed with cilantro, olive oil and lemon; a white crescent of basmati rice; a swirl of carrot and red pepper coulis.

"What is this, a *Gourmet* magazine cover?" exclaims Eleanor. Ruta sighs at the simple pleasure of having someone cook her a meal. Bruce uncorks a box of Hochtaler wine, pours a glass for everyone except Greg, who motions at his non-alcoholic beer with mock sadness and rolls his eyes.

"Fake beer, seventeen different kinds of vitamins, Chinese herbs. You'd think I was a lesbian. . . . "

"You *are* a lesbian," says Bruce reassuringly.

"You should be doing creative visualization, too," says Eleanor, wagging her finger. "It helped Nina's breast cancer, there's no reason to think it couldn't help you. I have this book. . . . "

Bruce gently places a hand on Eleanor's mouth.

"Honey, put a lid on it." He holds up his glass. "To the chef, to the guests, to Chinese herbs, to *life.*" He waves one arm, bows deeply in Greg's direction, clinks his wine glass against Greg's can of Moussy beer. Greg turns to toss the salad, fusses over the three-berry pie in the oven, muttering to himself about this new crust recipe he tried.

Greg is a centrifugal force around which they gather, dispensing food and Newfoundland charm with practised skill. Ruta is reminded of her Baba, the way Greg anxiously scans their faces for expressions of pleasure while they tear into the food.

Eleanor is delivering a lecture on breast cancer and its analogies with the AIDS crisis.

"One out of five women have it, that's an even greater statistic than AIDS, especially if you look at it over time. If it was happening to men there'd be huge demos on the street, there'd be an ACT UP for people with breast cancer. . . . "

"PBCS," muses Bruce, his mouth full of basmati. "Sounds rather . . . lethal."

"It *is* lethal. You should see what Nina has to go through, today I had to go with her to get a body scan. . . . "

Ruta shoots Eleanor a look. Eleanor blinks, and gets it. She looks down sheepishly.

"More salad, girlfriend?" says Bruce sweetly.

"So, ah, how was it at the clinic today?" asks Ruta, putting one hand on Eleanor's back, the other on Greg's knee. Eleanor leans vulnerably into her touch. Greg moves briskly away to make coffee.

"Well, my favourite part is the waiting room," he says. "I cruise the guys who've been HIV positive for years, they know more than the doctors ever will. Anyways, I've decided to dump the AZT. I hate it. Doctor *Kildare* didn't agree, but. . . . " Greg stops suddenly. His face, for just a second, is naked with fear.

"Oh, fuck, I don't wanna talk about it. Anyone for my new Carpenters' album?"

Soon they are swaying around the room to "Close to You," lip-synching the words as Greg dons his long black wig. They are bent double laughing, except for Eleanor, who broods and chain smokes and leaves early.

"So what's with her?" demands Bruce while he studiously rolls a joint.

"Ah, we're in that slippery lover-slash-friend transition phase, and she's really worried about Nina and I want attention too and then there's Greg. . . . "

"Honey, if Eleanor's got someone else to try her creative vision-aryism with, it's *peachy* with me."

"Visualization."

"Whatever."

Bruce looks up from his task, peers at Ruta.

"So what's happening with you, babe?"

"I sleep. I eat, I go to a million meetings, I come home, I read books about depression and chronic fatigue, you know the kind, rainbows on the cover, daily affirmations, sappy poems. . . . "

"Chinese herbs?"

"Nah, that's Greg's department."

"Are you gonna take a holiday or something?"

"What, and leave little Greggie alone with *you*? Forget it."

"Aw, honey." Greg puts his arms around her, twirls her around the room. Karen Carpenter croons.

The next week, Greg is in hospital with pneumonia. They take turns sneaking in home-cooked meals: Ruta's Thai noodles, Eleanor's orange-glazed chicken, Bruce's Newfoundland Meatloaf with Campbell's Soup Sauce. Although their leather jackets bulge with obvious transgressions, they are never turned away. But Greg has no appetite for food, just bad 70s music, Madonna posters and his friends cracking jokes non-stop: food and humour a desperate offering to appease the howling wind at the hospital door.

Your dreams change. They are about small things. Your life narrows down. Subtle gestures of friendship, learned and then forgotten, become necessary again. Nuances of emotion, significant details about someone who is gone that now loom large in your waking hours. Irises in the middle of winter. The smell of cilantro. An old message on your phone machine that you don't erase. Although these things are not enough – because nothing is enough – they help to keep all of you alive.

Ora climbs onto Ruta's back, Zoe unties her running shoe laces, Nathan cries from the other room. No one seems to be actually watching "Sesame Street" so Ruta casually reaches for the remote and switches to "Entertainment Tonight."

"*Hey man!* Whaddya think you're doin'?" bellows Ora good-humouredly as she lands from the back of the couch on Ruta's lap, grabs the remote and switches back to "Sesame Street" with practised six-year-old skill.

"*Awesome,*" yells Zoe, who has just started senior kindergarten and needs to show off his new repertoire of slang.

Nathan is still crying. Ruta, who was raised on Dr. Spock, plans to give him five more minutes. But before she can say not to, Ora plucks the baby out of his crib and strolls into the living room, cooing and singing to him, one eye on the TV.

"Pee pee!" says Zoe.

"You have to pee, honey?"

"No, silly. Nathan gone pee pee!" Zoe points, giggling, at Nathan's soaking diaper.

Ruta locates a bag of Huggies under the couch. Ora hands Nathan over and Ruta places him on a blanket on the floor. Ora and Zoe sit down cross-legged beside Ruta and watch curiously as she fiddles with the diaper. Zoe whispers something to Ora. They chuckle.

"Don't you know how to change a *diaper?* " asks Ora, amazed.

"Well, ah, I'm sure I can figure it out somehow. . . . "

Zoe slaps his knee and chortles: "Too much!"

Ora emits a long-suffering sigh, takes the diaper and briskly folds it around Nathan in efficient origami folds, burbling baby talk at him all the while. Nathan's face relaxes, he gurgles with delight.

"It's okay, " says Ora, patting Ruta on the back. "Everyone has to learn sometime." Zoe winks and gives Ruta a thumbs-up sign.

Nathan falls asleep almost immediately. Zoe is lured to bed with ghost stories and Ora is convinced to get into her flannel nightie and grizzly bear slippers. She finagles her way back to the living room, insists on watching "Street Legal" and dozes off during the news, her head on Ruta's lap. Ruta carries her to bed. Ora wakes up for a moment, leans forward with a sleepy outstretched hug, then falls dramatically back into the bed.

Dawn gets home at 2:30 A.M., her face aglow with adventure: the Boncongonista's on Queen Street; a speak at an artist's loft in Parkdale; a ride home with a poet named Djimi who kissed her goodnight and pressed a joint into her hand, which Dawn and Ruta now companionably share. Ruta is slightly nauseous from too much TV. She closes her eyes, leans back and listens while Dawn describes her evening, then segues into strategy about next week's action in front of the police station.

"You know, I cried for an hour after I heard," Dawn says. "It could have been Ora shot down. Hell, it could have been me. That woman was practically my age. It's gotten so I'm afraid to send the kids to the corner store, this neighbourhood is crawling with cops. . . . "

Ruta opens her eyes, rubs Dawn's shoulders.

"Look, I'll do a phone-around tomorrow to the Women's Action Coalition," says Ruta. "If you have some posters I could put them up at the bars, too. I mean, we got 500 women to the December 6th rally, maybe we can get it into their heads that it's the same thing. . . . "

Dawn smiles weakly, ruffles Ruta's hair, stands up, takes a deep breath.

"Look, honey. The shooting of Sofia Cooke is about racism, y'hear? You can make all the connections you want, but you gotta know it's not the same thing. Racism is the main thing here, girl, the bottom line."

Ruta does not reply. Dawn shivers suddenly, picks up the bag of Huggies, dumps it behind the couch, goes to the kitchen and puts on water for tea. She comes back and stands in the doorway.

"By the way. I heard about Greg," she says. "I'm really sorry."

"Yeah, well, we knew he was gonna die. It's just that gay men keep going to the last minute, you know, doing AIDS benefits and drag queen turns, so you can never really imagine them dead. It's okay. Maybe he's better off up there in fag heaven, with all the boys from New York. Me 'n Eleanor are getting along better since. . . . I think it's bringing us closer together, you know. . . . "

Ruta starts to cry and Dawn sits beside her, holding her hand until she's finished. It's the first time Ruta has cried since the memorial service. They stay up for another two hours drinking herbal tea and trading crazy ideas and political visions. Dawn confides in Ruta her dream of a resource centre for single mothers, by 4 A.M. they have it fully funded and furnished. Ruta falls asleep on the couch, wakes up early to the sound of Nathan crying, slips quietly out of the house. The sky is pink and mauve with dawn.

In the dream and out of it, you're running scared.

You're doing what you've always done, you organize. You respond to this, strategize about that. You write letters, circulate petitions, chair meetings, type up minutes, strike subcommittees, write briefs, make presentations, stage actions on the street. You organize: panel discussions, film screenings, rallies, demos, information tables, educational forums, marches, sit-ins, die-ins, speak-outs. Feminism, lesbianism, race, class: multiple oppressions mean multiple meetings. Your phone machine crackles with reminders, obligations, need. You're swimming against a current whose source you're hardly certain of anymore. Someone asks you what it is you've achieved and you have no answer.

You stop. Maybe for a year, maybe for five. Your back goes out or your girlfriend starts sleeping around or someone dies. A crisis brings you back to who you are. You change cities, hardly anyone notices you're gone. Maybe it's true what your mama said: "Those politics will continue without you. Rest or go on vacation, you won't change the world, others have tried and failed."

You realize you weren't so indispensable after all.

"Ruta, you're *not* going to wear that shirt with *those* pants, are you? I mean, like, that's *totally* uncool."

Ruta's hand freezes halfway between eyeliner and eyelid. No one in Toronto ever called her Ruta, everyone there took the easy way out, translated her name Anglo-style: Ruthie.

Christa's face appears in the bathroom mirror, smiling triumphantly.

"I have just the thing. . . . "

"Chrissie, gimmee a break. My knees haven't been seen in public since 1965."

"1965," muses Christa. "I was *born* in 1965. . . . " She is pensive for five seconds and then rouses herself back into fifteen-year-old hyper-space. "Anyways, it's in your closet so you must have worn it *once.*"

"It's, er, someone else's."

"Oh yeah? *Who?* " Christa pushes her own face into the mirror's reflection, one eyebrow raised in a mock leer.

"Eleanor. An ex-lover."

"Oh, you *lezz*bians," moans Christa, rolling her eyes. "You *lezz*bians and your thousands of ex-lovers." She flounces out of the bathroom.

When Ruta emerges, made up and ready for a night at the Kiev Bar, she sees Christa languid on the couch, flipping through a copy of *Fireweed,* sipping a coke, sneakered feet propped on the wall. In her role as Christa's adoptive aunt, Ruta is secretly delighted by Christa's teenage insouciance. Christa looks up.

"Ruta, can I ask you something?"

"Sure, hon'. Anything," lies Ruta. She sits down warily in the rocking chair. She's hoping it won't be a sequel to the quiz on safe sex and the physics of heterosexual penetration she bluffed her way through last summer. Although Christa probably knows more about het sex than Ruta ever will, it seems she still needs to feign innocence. Ruta complies and they enact a mother-daughter scenario that tension between Christa and her mom – Ruta's childhood friend, Elise – won't allow. Meanwhile, Ruta racks her brain for remnants of health class information, sneaks looks at *Our Bodies, Our Selves* and tries to hide the astonishment and pure worry that floods her as Christa becomes a sexual being. Christa interrupts her thoughts.

"Ruta, did you hear what I asked you?"

"No, sweetie, what?"

"At what age do you become lesbian? I mean, like, how do you *know*? Like, can you be lesbian at my age?"

"Sure. Some people know ever since they're little. Some don't know until they're sexually active and others, like me, don't come out until we're in our 20s. And for some women, it's much later."

Ruta throws in a bit of political rhetoric for good measure.

"If it were accepted in society, we wouldn't worry about when. I mean, was there a time when you actually *decided* you were heterosexual?"

"Well, that's just the thing. I don't think it's so black and white. Like, just because I sleep with guys, that doesn't mean I can't sleep with girls, right?"

Ruta has been so careful not to proselytize, she hadn't considered this possibility.

"Anyways, I think I'd like to have a relationship with a girl some day. I think it would be really beautiful."

Christa goes back to her magazine. Ruta stares out at the shadow of the mountain, dark against the purple night sky. She can hear Brian upstairs, giggling, then Yves' low voice and then a two-tone peal of laughter. She turns to Christa.

"Hey, kiddo, I'm a good influence on you, don't you think?"

Christa closes the magazine, throws it on the floor, sits up, stretches, yawns.

"Yeah, Ruta, I guess you are . . . hey you know what? I think we should have some kinda legal ceremony, so you could be my *legal* aunt. Wouldn't that be cool?"

There's a grin on Christa's face, she's joking, but she's wistful too, wanting reassurance to bridge the sudden gulf of difference. Ruta goes over to the couch, gives Christa a hug.

"But honey, we're already family. Who needs legal bills?"

Family. Familiar. *Familia:* the word Baba uses, a slavicized English word, a Ukrainian that is almost dialect, its original form long since lost.

Family: the word lesbians use, for close friends, for lovers, for community. For Ruta, there has always been something missing in this construct: a smell, a certain slant of light. A shared history, a continuity, a cadence of language impossible to describe. A completeness she has rarely seen but one she will recognize when she does.

Eleanor was family, so were Greg and Bruce. And then they weren't. Greg was dead, Bruce had withdrawn from everyone, she and Eleanor hardly had any contact these days. Was it only family that could outlast a pain so deep it made you want to push away the people you loved most in the world?

Maybe she needed a different word for Eleanor and Bruce and

Christa, one that didn't yet exist. Maybe that was part of the problem.

She goes to the city where her grandmother lives, a work trip intercut with family obligation. She has not seen her Baba or her brother, sister and nieces in five years. There are frantic taxi rides across town to get to Baba's for dinner, then back to the conference. To add to the confusion, she meets a woman and speeded-up conference courtship rituals begin.

They're getting coffee in the hallway during a tedious panel discussion, and the coffee urns are empty.

"Oh, shit, the coffee urns are empty," says Ruta.

"Oh dear," says the other.

They go to a dim coffee shop across the street and miss the next two panels. The woman's name is Zena. She suggests they have dinner.

"I can't," replies Ruta. "I have to be at my grandmother's by seven. She's making cabbage rolls, just for me."

"Well, how about breakfast tomorrow?"

"Brunch at my aunt's and then there's the closing plenary."

"Right, wouldn't want to miss that."

"No. . . . "

Zena sighs, flips through her *Everywoman's Almanac*.

"How's Monday?"

"That's Halloween."

"Ummhmm. . . . "

"I promised my sister I'd help with the kids' costumes and go trick-or-treating and after that we're meeting up with my brother. It's a bar reunion of sorts. . . . "

"Look, it's okay," says Zena, closing her almanac with a snap.

"Well, why don't we spend Monday day together? I'd love to go to . . . the zoo."

"The zoo?"

"Yeah, the Storyland Valley Zoo. I used to go there as a kid."

To Zena's relief, the zoo is closed on Mondays, so instead they drive to a frozen lake in Zena's car. They walk along brown, frost-crisped paths, tell each other childhood stories, exchange home-grown theories about all the big issues: coming out, non-monogamy, sex. Ruta is glad when the conversation finally turns to what kind of sexual practise they're into, because they're halfway around the lake and she has to be back in the city by five.

"Everyone here talks about this and that," surmises Zena, "like s/m, butch/femme, but no one will actually admit to doing any of it. You'd think all we did was sit around and hold hands."

"You have lovely hands." It's the best line Ruta can think of, it's already three.

By six, they are on the highway going 100 miles per hour. Zena's knuckles are white on the steering wheel but there's a contented smile on her face. Ruta's mind is racing. It's time she came out to her family but in the meantime, she figures out a scheme. Ruta will pretend to have left her bag in Zena's car. She will suddenly re-member this at the bar and will be driven to Zena's where she will pick up her bag. And stay the night.

The evening is a whirlwind of pleasurable fragments, impossi-ble to fit together: her nieces' delighted faces as she paints them blue, red, yellow and green; her smallest niece, Irena, holding tight to Ruta's hand as she trick-or-treats for the first time; later, her awkward brother buying her a cocktail at the bar; the musky smell of her fingers as she picks up her glass; reminiscing with her sister about long-forgotten episodes: the summer trips to Banff, the treasure hunts at Baba's; the lingering sensations of sex all through her body.

She doesn't make it to Zena's till 1 A.M. and is asleep ten minutes later. They spend the next morning frantically making love and Ruta catches an afternoon flight home. Despite huge differences, geographical and others, they remain lovers for two years. Apart from Zena's charm, Ruta thinks this is because Zena accompanies her to Baba's house, allows Baba to kiss her three times on alternating cheeks and to feed her impossible amounts of *varenyky*, cabbage rolls and borscht, without complaint. While Ruta sits, beaming, between them, watching a completeness she didn't know she was even looking for.

Familia. Familiar and strange, lover and family, both at the same time.

Your life takes you places you didn't plan to go. You are awake in the middle of the night. You have no dreams.

Ruta and Zena break up, Ruta's friends have expected it, awaiting the news with a thin-lipped sense of inevitability. The friends refrain from saying 'we told you so,' but they do say it is *just as well*, because long-distance relationships don't make you happy, because Ruta has 'intimacy issues,' because Zena is the daughter of an alcoholic and therefore afraid of forming close ties. The friends read her excerpts from self-help books and daily affirmation books, over the phone.

But Ruta *had* been happy. Visiting Zena, she had found home again, or something that felt like home.

The breakup does not go well. Ruta is mature and self-actualized with Zena over the phone and then sends letters she is not proud of. For several weeks, she is unable to get out of her bathrobe and fuzzy slippers. The friends stop phoning. Ruta's behaviour does not fit what the self-help books have predicted.

Only Brian is able to provide occasional refuge for her broken heart, knocking on her ceiling regularly at five for cocktails. Together they watch the sun set over the mountain, sipping dry martinis, listening to Frank Sinatra, Brian silently handing over Kleenex and Ritz crackers with cheese.

For months, she travels through this grief. It does not take long for her to realize the pain is no longer about Zena. She is mourning something long and huge, something that began before she met Zena or even Greg, something that disappeared before he did. It is something that needs to come back, something connected with spirit, though Ruta would never say that to any of her friends, even Eleanor, who has discovered Feminist Spirituality and goes to meetings with women who have stars, rainbows and unwieldy-sounding goddesses in their names.

For the first time in her life, Ruta becomes resigned to, then accustomed to and finally comfortable with, being alone. She often goes to the gay and lesbian bookstore on a Friday to buy a book for the weekend, which she hungrily devours whole, like a loaf of bread. As an experiment, she turns off her answering machine for a week and survives.

Aloneness falls around her body like a snake, coiled, inexorably, across her chest and her stomach. This was her project: to tame the beast, to learn the habit of aloneness, to embrace the snake. Just as she and the snake become long-lost friends, her phone machine begins to twinkle again and a woman finds her way into Ruta's life. Ruta does not need this woman, which is exactly the point. This woman is inevitable. No games or courtship manoeuvres occur. Ruta is nearing the end of her passage through grief and this woman holds Ruta when she cries.

The snake returns sometimes, after the woman has left. It slowly makes its way to Ruta's bed. It coils itself around her stomach at odd times, like three in the morning or midnight, and keeps Ruta

THE WOMAN WHO LOVED AIRPORTS

awake, thinking. She thinks about Greg, who died five years ago, about Yves, who shot himself last month at dawn, in the middle of Carré St. Louis. She thinks about Nina, who lost all her hair, and about her father, who is about to have heart surgery. She thinks about Zena, whom she no longer knows. There are no dreams.

The woman plans to move in with Ruta. Ruta does not protest, though she does ask for more time, a delay, a stay of intimacy. But the woman is as determined and as soft-moving as the snake. And the woman is tender. She says to Ruta: "I want to make a life with you."

Ruta will always be alone inside herself. But there is someone in her life who has said she will be at home whenever Ruta gets there. Ruta knows enough to recognize this as a gift that must not be turned away.

Baba has not yet met this woman but Ruta hopes she will. Baba is still asking her about Zena, saying: "She vas nice gerrl, how come she don't visit no more?" Ruta changes the subject, wishes Baba could meet Brian, Bruce and Christa, too. On Christmas Eve at Baba's, Ruta sets an extra place setting for the dead, the way Baba says they did in the Old Country, so that Greg and Yves can be there with them.

You are sitting at a long table with all your friends from different places and times. It is Sviat Vechir – *Christmas Eve – a night when magic things occur.*

Your ex-lover from Toronto, whom you haven't spoken to in years, is there. She leans across the table to talk to your non-biological niece, whose face catches the light, eyes burning with all the fierceness and energy of her nineteen years. Your friend who died five years ago sits next to her. His face is clear, his eyes are bright. He sits quietly and watches, holding onto the fragile threads of friendship that spark across the room. Your grandmother ladles borscht into his bowl and tells him he's too thin. He laughs, says he never felt better. They compare technique; your grandmother, aghast, has never met a man, let alone a Newfoundlander, who could cook borscht.

Your straight-but-sensitive childhood friend huddles in conversation with your upstairs neighbour and his ex-lover, who died last month. They are discussing his New Year's drag queen outfit and what stockings to wear with his sequined dress. Your best friend, the one you thought you had lost, sits beside you. She is sharing a joke with the daughter of a friend, now a seemingly mature thirteen-year-old. Later, you catch the child sneaking sips of wine, a time-honoured Christmas tradition. You let it go, but your neighbour slips away to the dépanneur to get ginger ale. Some women from the anti-poverty collective are here, comparing statistics with your other ex-lover, the social worker from Edmonton, who winks at you when the conversation gets too grim.

Your aunt from Ukraine, now 98 years old, stands in an apron at the stove, stirring the mushroom sauce, humming national anthems. Your lover catches your eye and silently toasts to your health. Your grandmother fills your bowl with soup.

The windows glow with blue light. Occasionally, animals appear behind the panes of glass. They have special powers, their eyes are yellow and knowing. Inside the house, the future and the past are held within the present, for just one night. Many languages are spoken and all are understood.

You sit in the midst of this. You are happy. Your people are the people you love.

Food / *Yizha*

I⊤'s DARK, *that heavy woollen darkness that descends in November after everyone turns their watches back one hour. The cabbage leaves are slippery to the touch as Ruta takes them out of the refrigerator and realizes she needs to turn the light on, though it's only 5 P.M.*

She arranges things on the kitchen table: pot of rice, plate for rolling, baking dish. She sits down and begins filling cabbage leaves with rice, in a sequence of gestures learned in childhood. It's a bit like rolling a joint, thinks Ruta. Spoon the mound of rice onto the end of the leaf, roll the leaf away from yourself and then tuck the ends in. Place the cabbage rolls snugly next to each other inside the baking dish. The routine is soothing and also mindless. Time passes.

The women are eating apple cheesecake in the tiny Czech café on McKay Street. It is November, mid-afternoon. Ruta sits alone, delaying her errands with a *café allongée*. She pretends to read a magazine but her eyes continually return to the cheesecake-eating women. Prokofiev plays in the background. The women speak Ukrainian. They lean towards one another with relaxed elbows.

A woman from behind the pastry counter – Ruta supposes she is Czech – goes over to the women at the table. They are middle-aged, the Czech woman looks about 65. She says something. Ruta strains to listen. She can only understand fragments of this Czech/Ukrainian mix but she knows they are talking about history, the war and the recent changes. She hears the word *chudoh,* which means miracle.

The Ukrainian women are serious and then they laugh, delighted that they are somehow able to understand the Czech woman. They plead with her to sit down and join them. The Czech woman is embarrassed, wipes her hands on her apron and walks away. The Ukrainian women are confused. Then the Czech woman returns with the tray of the remaining cheesecake and a bottle of brandy, which she opens with mock secretiveness, looking over her shoulder as though she is an undercover agent. Some of the women laugh and their laughter is contagious. They slap their knees, wipe tears out of their eyes, shake their heads and proceed to finish off the entire cheesecake and drink all the brandy, their languages spinning around them in extravagant confusion.

Ruta pays for her coffee and asks for a slice of apple cheesecake to go. She pauses for a moment by the women's table, wanting to say something in Ukrainian but her language is stuck in her throat.

Later at home, Ruta finds she is suddenly very hungry. She eats the piece of cheesecake but it is not enough. It is a hunger with no end, which no amount of food can satisfy.

Never enough, never enough, the words are always in her head.

"Never satisfied," Colleen would say, shaking her head. Ruta used to visit Colleen in Kingston. Colleen was, well, there wasn't a word for what Colleen was. A weekend sex-pal, a soulmate, a girlfriend in the true sense of the word: one who sits cross-legged on your bed, listening to your most secret of secrets. Colleen and Ruta would get together, they would talk, hug, talk and make love until dinnertime. That was when the arguments began.

It was usually about 6 P.M. when Ruta would raise her head from Colleen's lovely orange pubis and say: "Whaddya wanna do for dinner?"

"Oh, I dunno," Colleen would say. "What you're eating right now is keeping me pretty happy." Or words to that effect. And so Ruta, loving Colleen as she did, would bend her head back to her task, patiently waiting for Colleen to come, which took 45 minutes to an hour. Ruta was very attentive but the truth of the matter was, she was thinking about dinner the whole time she was going down on Colleen.

Chinese food take-out? Nah, we should go out, we've been in this room all day. Maybe I'll cook something, the gado-gado chicken, if we leave soon, we could get to the supermarket before it closes. There's romaine in the fridge, I could make a caesar salad and there's the cookies I brought. We could always go to a restaurant, some place special, with candlelight and soft music and pretty yuppie food....

"Earth to Ruta.... *Honey,* you've been licking that same spot for ten minutes."

"Oh. Oh, sorry. Did you come?"

"Yes, 20 minutes ago."

"Oh. Whaddya wanna do for dinner? Wanna go out?"

"Let's just stay in. I'd be happy with a baked potato or something. I'm really not that hungry."

With that, Colleen would bend her head to Ruta's breasts and suck Ruta's nipples with exquisite precision, her long red hair like a silk scarf on Ruta's shoulders, her fingers sweet along Ruta's labia until Ruta came and came and came.

"So, whaddya wanna do for dinner, ya wanna go out?" Ruta would ask afterwards.

"Never satisfied," Colleen would sigh. "*Never* satisfied."

Ruta would then infer cultural intolerance on Colleen's part and Colleen would imply that Ruta had intimacy issues or, worse, boredom issues, which made Ruta feel guilty and act defensive. They would argue until they were tired and all the restaurants in Kingston were closed, then Colleen would bake some potatoes or they would order pizza, after which they'd go to bed, exhausted.

"I used to be food-centred like you," says a tall, delicate-featured woman named Fiona to Ruta at the lesbian solstice retreat. "But not anymore. I got over it."

Fiona sighs, rises gracefully and lopes to the kitchen to get a second helping of the five-course Ukrainian meal Ruta has brought for Christmas Eve. Solstice is fine but Christmas Eve is what resonates with Ruta, finds her making borscht and cabbage rolls like her life depends on it. Which, in a spiritual way, it does. As the red earthenware dish had filled with green cabbage leaves a few days earlier, she and her friend Larissa had sung along to her scratchy Ukrainian Christmas carol record, sipping brandy as they stuffed the *holubtsi*. And Ruta had thought to herself: *I have continued my traditions, I have survived.*

This thought recurs to her after Fiona leaves the room. Ruta toys with the idea of telling her about peasant traditions, which are never traditions at the time they are created but are literally a way to stay alive. Which are about how women make themselves visible in history, which are about speaking even when you are not given voice.

She thinks about what it is to be English in this country ("I'm not English, I'm *Canadian,*" Fiona had retorted in an earlier conversation). Fiona's been deprived of her history, too. Only the English were called white or even Canadian, way back when. If you were anyone else, you were foreign, you were alien or you were Indian – and therefore under suspicion, just for speaking your language, eating your own food. Fiona probably wouldn't know about internment camps, pass laws and lynch mobs made up of English men. It's all been erased from the history books and innocence is the only thing that's been passed on.

English, Canadian, Anglo-Saxon: it's a subtly colourless identity, and the phantom centre of power is always invisible. Ruta is always apologizing for even naming it, when really she makes room for it, she effaces herself in it, she feeds it, feeds it, all the time.

But instead she says nothing and goes to get more food.

When Ruta was a kid, her mama was always on a diet so that, at suppertime, there would be something like beef goulash with sour cream in one pot and boiled vegetables in another. Ruta's mama ate only the vegetables. Even now, when Ruta visits, her mama will look appraisingly at her and say: "You've put on weight" or "You've lost weight." Either way, there will be the two pots and Ruta feeling bad for going for the goulash and not the boiled cabbage. Ruta has weighed the same for the past fifteen years.

Ruta is her Baba's daughter. There is food no matter what time of day or night Ruta visits, nothing fancy but a lot of it, and Baba, like everyone's Ukrainian cliché, saying: *"Yizh, yizh"* ("eat, eat") as Ruta eats and eats. The food is simply the backdrop for Baba's stories, which she unwinds slowly: the long juicy story about crossing the Atlantic in '33, the short bittersweet anecdotes about prairie life during the Depression, or the spicy contemporary melodramas about blackmarketeering relatives from Ukraine, arriving on

Baba's doorstep with no money and big ideas about smuggling VCRs. Ruta sits and listens and eats, feeling the time with Baba ease away like slow-motion sand in an hourglass.

"*Mebbe dis be last time I see you,*" says Baba every time they say good-bye, but Ruta always believes there will be more food and more stories. Although there is not enough time or money to go to Baba's city as often as she would like, Ruta leaves satiated. She leaves with something she will both hold onto and pass on, a magic kind of food that expands with time.

She pulls the cabbage rolls out of the oven. The edges of the leaves are crisp but the holubtsi *themselves are moist and plump, just like her mama's. Except that Mama would probably say:* You don't cook big things like that just for yourself, *and Ruta is pulling out one plate, a knife and fork and some sour cream, placing them on the table. She lights a candle. She sits at the table. She eats.*

Mama, *Donya*

SHE MAKES COFFEE in the morning, makes it while I'm still asleep, so it's not like I actually see her doing it, or can tell it's for me. But it's always there, in the old glass percolator, strong, the way I like it, stronger than she'd drink it herself. Sometimes she joins me as I sit on the couch, the faded floral one in the family room covered with embroidered pillows from Aunt Ruta in Ukraine. We gaze out the window to the backyard and sip our coffee, not talking. The silence of the house is temporary, as is this wordless moment of truce between us. My spiritually inclined friend Eleanor would call it 'being in a state of grace.' In it, we are briefly fixed in time and know our names: mama, *donya*; mother, daughter.

Sometimes when I'm visiting, but not always, my father wakes me for his special breakfast: buckwheat kasha. The smell is powerful, it represents childhood and being cared for. My father gives me a generous serving, with milk and salt, the way we always ate it, and I don't tell him I never eat kasha anymore. He watches me fondly as I force it down and then the sweet milk of his attention runs dry and he's gone, to his books and his study, leaving me with my mother again.

We go shopping. It's a form of recreation in a life clipped and narrowed by respectability and the demands of a husband's career, so I comply. I grab some Tylenol 3 and a hefty copy of *Canadian Woman Studies* journal in case I get stranded in some remote corner of the Piney Grove Mall. All of these malls are named after geographical features that no longer exist: huge, bloated structures that capture women with what my friend Brian calls their "lobster trap architecture."

The voices of my friends are particularly eloquent today, evidence of sagging resolve at the halfway point of my ten-day visit. I have made a pact with my superego: no remarks about American imperialism while watching TV, no feminist rhetoric as I read the morning paper. I have brought a small but weighty library of socialist-feminist literature that I will never read, some lesbian trash romance (for balance) and, for desperate moments, a couple of languorous, syrupy new age relaxation tapes Eleanor got me the last time I had bad PMS. And I will call Claire. But only once. I don't want to get too addicted and, besides, with Baba gone and buried just one month ago, I can give them ten days of my life. It's nothing to me, it's everything to them. This is the mantra I repeat to myself as we stroll in a leisurely fashion through the imitation-pine innards of the Piney Grove Mall.

She wants to buy me a dress. It's not bad, a simple flowery print, 100 percent cotton, a flattering cut. She's always had good taste. I tell her I have nowhere to wear such a dress and her pleasure fades. We go for a coffee to the Forest Glen Café. She starts to tell me about Nadia, the daughter of a friend of hers. She thinks I will be able to relate: Nadia is the newly-elected president of the Conservative Party Women's Caucus in town.

I nearly choke on my cinnamon-blueberry danish. Nadia and I used to have elaborate, delicious sleep-overs, sneaking contraband cigarettes out on the back porch and reading *Cosmopolitan* together in bed. We'd pore over articles like "Masturbation: Everywoman's Guide" and "How to Let Your Man Get You." We might as well have been reading the collected works of Margaret Mead, for all the relevance this stuff had to our regulated suburban lives. Somehow, in our neighbourhood library, we discovered Betty Friedan and consecrated ourselves to the distant, downtown Women's Liberation Movement. We were all of sixteen at the time. Nonetheless, I feel betrayed.

"Has Nadia joined R.E.A.L. Women yet?" I mutter. Mama looks away.

Strike two. One more and the hard-won truce is over. I tell her I've changed my mind about the dress and she buys it – $89.99, a month's grocery money for me. Also: black lace stockings and enormous silver earrings. It makes her happy, I reason. Maybe I'll give the dress to Christa for her birthday. We start walking to the car. Two women are in front of us, carrying groceries and walking close together, hips touching. I've never seen such a thing at the Piney Grove Mall. They must be from out of town. I can't take my eyes off of them. My mother is talking about the new extension to the mall over on Orchard Boulevard. The women get into the car across from ours. One of them leans over and kisses the other on the lips. They embrace. I'm four years old, watching something bad: enthralled, horrified, delighted. My mother notices them.

"Queers. They're all over the place these days," she says matter-of-factly, as though she's talking about raccoons, and starts the car. I can't imagine where she learned the word.

When we get home, she turns on the TV, then goes into the kitchen to start dinner. I ask if she needs any help but as usual she says no, so I sit in front of the television, near enough to the kitchen to indicate my solidarity. I am simultaneously watching a special called "Women of the World" – "a look at beautiful women and the fashions they wear" – and reading a book called *Labour Pains: Women's Work in Crisis*. I hear my mother softly humming muzak. For the moment, she and I are content. My father comes downstairs and puts on his favourite record: the Dnipro Men's Chorus singing Ukrainian war songs. My mother is chopping cabbage in unconscious time to a marching song. The three-track sound becomes too much and I dissolve into imaginative reveries about Claire – our last camping trip, and all the little love things she whispered in my ear before I left – until my mother calls me for dinner.

The television stays on all evening. A group of experts discusses The Deficit. They cannot decide whether medicare or old age pensions should be cut back but they do agree, quite jovially, that cultural funding should be the first to go, especially things like the obscene lesbian performance piece that played at the National Gallery last week.

"Hmph. Interesting. Those girls we saw at the mall . . . " says my mother while she ladles out the borscht, making some sort of associative, perhaps even empathetic, leap of the imagination.

"*Pffft,*" sneers my father. "Bestiality, nothing more."

I steer us to safer shores. Federal politics, the new right wing. My parents are solid liberals. We can bond about the pea-brain policies of Preston Manning. We scuffle mildly about whether the NDP is falling apart. We agree the Conservatives got too arrogant and I concede that the Liberals have it together as far as appearances are concerned.

Mostly, my father talks, my mother listens, or pretends to. I skip dessert and flee to the basement for a cigarette, still contraband after all these years. A picture of the Pope smiles at me from the wall, forgiving me my sins. Tomorrow, I will call Claire.

She has found an occasion for the dress. The next-door neighbours, the Watsons, have invited us to a big family dinner. We should be honoured, says my mother. They heard about Baba, they want to cheer us up.

I attempt a pleased smile, making a mental note to bring along the joint Brian thoughtfully slipped into my bag before I left. The Watsons are on the wrong side of a great many key social issues. He is a retired Canadian Air Force general. She is a homemaker and a volunteer for the local pro-life group, which regularly pickets the only abortion clinic in the city. Their son Chip studied communications on an army scholarship. He got married last month. Kitty Watson, divorced three years ago, will soon remarry Bud, who happens to be a born-again Christian. Everyone will be there.

Mama seems fascinated and pleased by all these curious, English goings-on. She fills me in on the breakages and repairs to the Watson family tree, and I make appropriate responses while I dress. The frock is becoming, though the stockings are a touch sleazy. I pluck some hairs out of my mole, paint on some eyeliner and sip a beer. My mother offers me jewellery. She thinks the eyeliner is too heavily applied. I sigh and rummage through her makeup bag for lipstick. No sense just going halfway.

Last year we argued bitterly about the Middle East. Before that, it was the fall of the Sandinistas. We're at dessert by the time General Watson and I loosen up. By some oversight, we've been seated next to each other. I realize my excessively seductive appearance has thrown him off. His eyes slip nervously and frequently to my black-lace thighs.

Mrs. Watson dishes trifle onto our cut-glass dessert plates. We are discussing The Media. Chip Watson is a radio announcer.

"I'm realizing how much power we as The Media have and it's scary," he says. "Take AIDS for example. The Media have virtually created an epidemic. People, ah, normal people, with children and families, are afraid, ah, afraid to be . . . sexual now."

Chip blushes suddenly. His new wife Deb coughs into her napkin. Mrs. Watson breathlessly offers coffee-or-tea. Everyone ignores her. Mr. Watson cuts in.

"AIDS is a homosexual disease, son, and let's not forget it. It's been foisted upon us by the perverted activities of a mob of child molesters. They should be lined up and shot."

I didn't plan it. It's just that my arm muscles and the innermost stirrings of my soul were suddenly, profoundly in synch. I lean over to get the cream and nudge a bottle of wine. A half-litre of red Kressman's lands in Mr. Watson's lap.

"Terribly sorry," I mutter. "I'm feeling rather dizzy. I really must go."

I gather my things and leave. I smoke the joint on the back porch of my parents' house, in silent homage to Nadia, circa age sixteen. I listen to the distant wail of ambulance sirens. I think about Baba. I suddenly feel so sad.

"Why did you do it, Ruta?" she asks the next morning.

"Do what?" I reply, rather indignantly.

She doesn't answer. It's rare that I can really put one past my mama. So I discard the speech I had prepared on premenstrual syndrome and how it can lead to violence and sometimes murder. Besides, my reserve of sweet submissiveness has just about run out.

"Watson is a racist sexist jerk. I'm sick of hearing him froth at the mouth like that, year after year after year. It's people like him who kill off peasants in Central America. He makes me sick, he makes me feel stupid, and besides, he baits me. . . . "

"What do you mean he *baits* you? He was talking about *homosexuals*. Why do you have to jump up and defend every cause on this earth? Why can't you just take care of your own?"

My mother is crying. I go over and put my arms around her, the way I would if it were Eleanor or Christa or Claire, trying to comfort, saying I'm sorry, expecting to be understood. But her back stiffens and she leaves the room.

I phone Claire that afternoon and tell her how I miss her touch, her woman-smell, her body warmth in our bed. I hear my voice speak soft and calm again. She in turn makes comforting sounds on the phone, shrieks with delight when I tell her about the Watson Episode, and tells me I must make peace with my mother. She arranges to meet my plane the next day.

It's a cold and drizzly morning, a perfect day for travelling. My father is getting ready to drive me to the airport, warming up the car. My mother has made kolbassa sandwiches wrapped in wax paper. She has placed a package of her poppyseed roll next to my bag.

I sit beside her on the couch. We are silent for several minutes, watching rain trail down the windows. I take her hand. Her fingers resist, curl in, but she doesn't pull away.

"Mama," I say, "I know you're sad now that Baba's gone. I'll be thinking about you. I'm going to call, every week. . . . "

She looks down at the floor.

"Rutechko," she whispers, "it was so long ago. Your Baba and Dido and me. Came such a long way from the Old Country. Now I've buried them both."

"I know, Mama. I know." I wipe a tear off her cheek and tell her I love her. She looks at me and smiles, almost imperceptibly. It is as though an old and brittle string wrapped around my heart has un-ravelled. I have never spoken like this to my mother before.

Halfway to the airport, my father clears his throat. Expecting his usual question, 'do you have enough money?' I turn to look at him with a smile on my face.

"Ruta. Who is this *Claire?*"

My heart sinks. My head spins.

"Claire who?"

"This girl you phone. Yesterday. I heard you."

"She's my . . . my Claire, ah, she's my friend."

"You, over 30, not married, no good job. It's not natural, how you live. Your mama so upset by you. How can you hurt her like that, how can you be such a. . . . "

Lesbian. The word has been hiding in my throat for days. Now it hangs in the air, unspoken, but so present.

"Acchh," he is saying. "What's the use. You stupid, stupid girl."

There is nothing more to say. All the provisional, first draft coming-out speeches were for later, much later, for a time when we would be wiser and closer. I had envisioned: slow recognition, a photograph developing more depth and, slowly, slowly, a familiar image again, the same picture, the three of us, same as before. But here there is nothing but shame and overexposure, artificial light in a private room.

We are at the airport. I have to check my baggage. The plane takes off in ten minutes. I grab my bags, lean over to kiss my father. He turns away, won't say a word.

Somehow I muddle through various line-ups and miraculously find myself on a plane, bald November fields dissolving into cloud cover, a long grey corridor for my thoughts to batter about like wingless birds, at the end of which is Claire and the liberated terri-tory of her strong, long woman's arms.

Claire comforts with glasses of wine, lengthy embraces, self-help books from the women's bookstore. They address various topics. She's not sure if I am mourning my dead grandmother, my estranged father or my oppressed mother. She came out to her parents long ago, over gin and tonics on some patio, and openly, easily, brings lovers home for Christmas.

"It's only a matter of time," she murmurs. "Wait til your mother meets me. She won't be able to resist my cooking, let alone my charm."

Although she never says so, it's clear she is bewildered by my grief. Claire is fifth-generation Canadian. Her parents call her 'dear,' play golf and eat strange things I've never touched, like Yorkshire pudding and tripe.

I tell her about my Baba, Kateryna, still unable to read or write in English when she died at age 88. Who came to Canada with my mother on a crowded, stinking boat to join Dido, my grandfather, who had fled the Polish Occupation. Who, whenever she said *doma* (home) meant a small village in Western Ukraine she hadn't seen in over 60 years. My Baba, a seamstress since she was sixteen, who wanted nothing more than to sew my wedding dress, whose pattern she had chosen years ago. And my mama, for whom grandchildren speaking to her in Ukrainian means continuity and future, the only genuine security she will ever accept in a country that daily makes her feel insecure.

I explain to Claire that, in Ukrainian, I am *samitna,* the word for unmarried which, coincidentally, sounds almost exactly like *samotna,* the word for lonely. And yet, in English, I am a lover, I am part of a community, I am a lesbian. *Lesbianka.* I cannot find that word in my Ukrainian dictionary. My mother tongue, no longer mother to me. And me, speaking, loving, working, in a tongue my own yet not entirely mine, estranged from origin.

Claire listens, is confused: by the whiteness of both our skins, by the common culture of our lesbianness. Worries I am overemphasizing difference. Then worries that difference, if it exists, separates. Somehow manages to learn a phrase or two in Ukrainian, surprises me with *Ya tebe lyublyu* (I love you). Buys me perogies and an Easter egg.

One night as we lie in bed, I try to describe the image I have of a stream with me in it, blocking its flow. The stream is my ancestry, the flow of tradition from one generation to the next. There seems to be no way of opening up this stream, so I am somehow always trapped in the present, my past there but closed off. A past only I can see, impossible for anyone, even Claire, to share.

This time she says nothing. She takes me in her arms, kisses me deeply and holds me until I fall asleep.

III

BODY JOURNEYS

Blue Video Night

THE TV MONITOR hovers in blue semi-darkness, my eyes transfixed by its flicker. Sixty different light patterns per second, each image lingering on my retina to merge into the other.

The woman's body I watch is nothing but illusion: willing collaboration between the visual system and the brain. (The product, really, of desire.)

It's 3 A.M. and I have to get out of this edit room. It's the time of night I make cuts I'll later regret: sudden, accidental colour shifts that result in green skin; twists in the narrative that result in tragedy. I don't feel in control.

I close my eyes and see the outline of her body.

It's early in the morning that my yearning for her rises from my skin. There is a salty smell, a tautness/wetness that happens when I remember how she pulled me towards her, my desire reaching down into my bones.

I put a different videotape into the deck. A close-up of waves – parody of B-grade romanticism – then the camera pulls back slo-mo to reveal a woman lying in the sand. The camera-woman

walks over to her, so there are bumpy shots of sand and tilted horizon. An anti-romantic shot of her feet, then the camera pans
across her body, mainstream cinema-style.

When the camera nears her face, I pause the machine. Her eyes
are closed, her lips are trying not to smile. Sometimes, all I can
remember are those lips, the sensuous mobility of her mouth, the
way it couldn't decide if she was serious or not, widening with pleasure or tightening with intensity. Which then leads me to contem-
plate her mouth sucking at my nipples, so serious and childlike,
then looking up at me with one of her enormous womanly smiles.
Or her mouth surrounding mine. Or her tongue in my cunt.

But in the video image her mouth is closed. I take my finger off
the pause button. The camera goes wide, to reveal her starting to
peel off her T-shirt.

It was just an experiment in home video porn, a joke, really.

Or, it was us performing our real selves. My desire to objectify
her. Her pleasure at being objectified, which she normally would
not reveal. The way it happens all the time, in the bars, at the
dances, all that looking and being looked at.

Yet she was, is, an active subject, too.

The camera wavers as the T-shirt hits the sand. There's no script,
there's only so many times you can pan back and forth, back and
forth, along a body. She starts to caress her own breasts, pulling at
her nipples. The camera zooms jerkily into extreme close-up,
focusses on the network of wrinkles forming around her nipple as it
becomes red and hard. None too steadily, the camera follows her
hand down to her crotch, she slips her hand into her wetness, pulls
it out and licks it very slowly. She smacks her lips, grins. The fram-
ing gets shaky here, from laughter or nervousness, I can't remember which. The horizon disappears. The sequence ends abruptly.

This isn't in the video:

She pulls me down onto the sand, suddenly, fiercely. Holds my arms down with one hand, explores my cunt with the other, her legs roughly pushing my thighs apart, her tongue loud around the contours of my ear, breathing into me until I'm dizzy. Her fingers persisting until her hand is inside of me and I cry out, her body hard and tough against me, all the while.

This isn't in the video either: how I fell, with such relief, head-long into her strength, me, a strong woman too. How I surrendered.

And there is no way of depicting this: her mind and body confronting my mind and body. The urgent pulse of our ideas. The heat.

Maybe I imagined it, this familiarity after years of otherness. She, like me, is an activist. She, like me, loves sex. The two have been so separate. The struggle had negated pleasure and pleasure had never seemed worth fighting for.

I frame her with my desire. I slow the image and examine her movements second by second, her lips time-lapsing into a smile. I manipulate her body, I have this power. I try to look at it, the hot centre of my attraction, but it is nowhere in these pictures, exists only in my body. There is no picture for this.

No, it's simply that we share the same political beliefs. She's against free trade, too. She's a feminist, too.

She's a woman, too. The edges of our bodies cup each other. Recognition made our eyes water, the first time we touched. And difference vibrates between us when we make love.

I'm sitting in this darkened edit room, looking at her electronically reproduced image. She's running towards the camera now in fake slo-mo – we're drawing heavily on melodrama here – but her face is illumined with a real happiness. I rewind the tape, she's getting further and further away.

I close my eyes. The flickering outline of her body, imprinted on my retina. They call this visual persistence. Or memory, so fragile it's hardly there at all.

The sequence ends. Snow (that's what they call it) fills the screen. Electronic snow, sizzling through blue video night.

The narrative waits for me to finish. There isn't much time left, the net is closing in. I want to depict this: a whole body, inscribed with my/her/our political and erotic meaning.

This body that exists only in fragments.

This story that survives, waiting for you/me to construct the ending I/we desire.

Small Wild Animals

MY MOTHER is afraid of only two things: embarrassment and mice. Once, when we were little, Mama had a lady friend over for tea. We were bored that day, so we decided to be the Truth Police.

"Have some more Upside-Down cake," said Mama to the lady.

"No thank you," said the lady, since it was obviously the last piece. "I've already had too much."

"Oh, go ahead," said Mama. "I've got plenty more."

"No you don't, Ma," I said. "That's the last piece."

My mama gave me one of her 'I'll get you later' looks, turned to the lady and laughed it off. Mama was having a good time and she was in a lying mood that day.

"Where's your husband?" asked the lady, brightly.

"Oh, he's at the office," replied Mama.

"No he's not, he's playing cards at the Ukrainian Hall," we chorused from the kitchen door where we were listening. A look of skepticism and confusion crossed the lady's face. And so it went. After the lady left, we got what we knew we deserved: a spanking and early bedtime.

But we had had a good time and so had Mama.

"Don't you dare embarrass me in front of someone like that again," she said.

We knew about the mice because Mama used to cry in her sleep. When we asked why, she said she had been dreaming about mice. My dad was never afraid of anything and he never, ever cried. We knew this because he said so.

So I was surprised when, last week, my mama told me he had cried for two days. Just like I was surprised when, idly, recently, I asked my mama: "Are you still afraid of mice?"

"Where did you get such a crazy idea," she sniffed. "I was never afraid of mice."

Lately, I've been dreaming about small, fragile animals: kittens tiny as mice and fish that flop weakly in the palm of my hand. I dream that these animals rely on me for their lives and that I have failed them miserably. I put them in the refrigerator where they freeze to death or I trip over them in the night and crush them senseless.

My father thinks he is dying. No one knows exactly when he will die: next month or next year or ten years from now. He goes to the hospital for regular stays, where he is loaded full of drugs that make his hands shake and his eyes go cloudy. He hates the food but he seems to enjoy the hospital environment. Perhaps here, in the clouds, he can forget. Dreams and ideas slip out of his shaky hands and leak away, through the hospital windows and into the humid summer air. The doctors do many tests and find more things wrong with him every day. The more wrong things they find, the more determined he is to live.

Often, I think I've done something wrong when really I haven't. I think someone has gone silent because of something I've said. Or I think nobody is happy because I haven't made enough food. So I forget about what I want or need and I tend to everyone until I think they are happy. I know I can always go away somewhere by myself and look after my own needs. Sometimes I wonder: where did I learn this? Why do I always feel I have to take care of fragile animals and people?

Whenever I visit my mother, the pattern is always like this: first we argue, then we eat and then there is a moment of tenderness before I leave. She kisses me in a tentative sort of way and gives me *varenyky* and fresh vegetables from her garden to take home. Lately, I've realized the food is a message. It says: *I want to be taken care of, too.*

What does it mean, to say you'll take care of someone?

A friend of mine is broke. Every weekend, she returns beer bottles to the store. Then she buys cigarettes and chicken wings. She proudly shows me the leftover pennies in her pocket. Alarmed, I give her my mother's vegetables, lend her money or buy her cigarettes or beer.

But lately, with my father ill, I'm overwhelmed. My skin feels tight and fragile. I tell my friend I need some taking care of, too. She can't or she won't. She gets angry over small things; finally, we lose touch.

So who takes care of the rescuer? Who parents the parent?

Back and forth to hospital I go, bearing presents that do not ease my father's pain: *varenyky* with sour cream stuffed into a tupperware container, fragrant pumpernickel bread, thick piles of *The New York Times* and *Der Spiegel*. The air is acrid with the smell of medicine and denial. My father's skin is grey. Occasionally, his eyes shine with a certain defiant light. One day, my friend Anna comes with me to the hospital and this inspires him to be a show-off. He sings "The Internationale" for us, in Ukrainian, from the edge of his hospital bed.

It seems my mother cares for me by giving me food, mountains of food: stuffed salmon, turkey, apple pie. All I can eat and more. *C'mon and eat,* she says, again and again. Usually, the meal runs late and I miss the bus I was going to catch home.

Food is power, food is an empire.

My latest dreams involve small, embarrassed accidents: blood on a bath towel, shit on a wall. Ugly secrets made public. Sometimes I want to tell my mama about these dreams and others. No, she's too vulnerable, I think.

How did you sleep? she asks when I visit. *Fine,* I say. Just fine.

I am afraid of small animals that run wild. I love camping but I shiver at the sight of the raccoons, rabbits and deer that always cross my path, as though drawn to my fear. Their eyes shine red, helpless and accusing in the dark rural nights. In the end, it's that combination of aggression and vulnerability that chills me.

Why can't they be one or the other? Why do they betray me as I run towards their small confiding voices, then find myself fleeing the teeth of their wide-open jaws?

Courage

MORNING, hard against my face. Toothpaste, shaving cream, after-shave. Some days, even the smell of a woman's cunt.

Other mornings are not like that. They are like this: my body, arching in anger or in lust. My voice on the phone, steady against the drone of bill collectors and magazine editors. My legs, pumping uphill on my bike or careening through the park on roller-skates. My hand crossing back and forth across a page, writing and re-writing my own body.

Mouth on her cunt, anyways.

Courage is a word to use carefully and seldom. But, still, it did take courage to keep making love, after the first flash flood of memory.

It takes courage to start talking. Me and Roslyn in a canoe in the middle of a lake in the Muskokas.

"You're *not* imagining it," says Roslyn, while she trails her fingers through the water. Or Shelley and Eva, in my living room one shrill-cold spring night, saying they'll take the bus with me out of town to visit my parents.

"You shouldn't have to do it alone," says Shelley as she pours the *tisane*. Or Simone, at Café l'Anecdote, on her way to the lawyer to press criminal charges against a family member who molested her 20 years ago, and afterwards, to get her hair cut: *"Quelque chose de différent."*

Life goes on, sometimes that's all courage is.

But courage sounds too Hollywood, too Ali McGraw in *Love Story,* too Canadian short-story, too Betty Ford.

Besides, not everyone was brave. Some women didn't want to hear about it, some women walked away, some women wouldn't or couldn't remember, some women continued the cycle of abuse. Onto other lovers, onto themselves.

Forget about courage. I want the telling to be matter-of-fact, compact, part of the everyday, the *quotidien.*

She holds me while I cry, rubs tears away with strong, calm hands. Then we continue, making love long into the morning, the light pale mauve behind the paper blind.

Later, she tells me what happened to her. I hold her as tightly as I can. After that, I fry eggs, make coffee, open the balcony window to the hot-yellow summer air.

Her smell is a demure and puzzling combination of musk and Head & Shoulders shampoo, interrupting the other smells, keeping me in the present instead of the past.

There are other smells. The smell of me, on her mouth. The dark green smell of the park across the street. The aroma of garlic and onion frying in olive oil: over and over again, we cook dinner for one another, a circle of women in a big city. We sit around kitchen tables and eat and tell elaborate funny stories. Barb always cooks from recipe books, always something special, we throw old Ukrainian epithets at each other, bent double laughing. She wags her finger as I choke on the laughter, says in Ukrainian, like her aunt does: *te budezh plakate*/you're going to cry, and finally I do, but it's not sad.

And mixed messages. The smell of bagels on St. Viateur, bicycling home in the dark, crackling open the paper bag for a midnight snack and suddenly I'm nauseous again and I recognize that yeasty smell, prickling my memory for months. Why is the smell of yeast so powerful and why do I always dream of my Baba's bread?

Some days, my sinuses are raw with blowing and smelling and blood.

"You're getting a cold," someone says.

"No, it's not a cold, it's something else," I say.

I say: *It's an epidemic of memory.*

Is it because of, or despite, this that I love sex, cruising women in and out of town, perfecting my lines?

"So, *dahling,* when are we going to have an affair?" I ask the woman in the red lipstick and tight black outfit. We're in an alleyway one hot June night, waiting to see some performance art. It feels like New York, but it's only Toronto, I'm quoting Sarah Schulman but I don't think she notices or cares. She laughs, rubs her fingers into the soft crevice between my shoulder and my neck, I sigh.

Without enough stories or pictures, sex becomes memory. I lie in bed alone and remember ways we've fucked. There was the time I leaned my back against her tight, small breasts and she fucked me with one hand, cradled me with the other. Like safety or like danger.

Sex is memory, going backwards into old sensations, staying present in the now, two women fighting pain, fighting the culture just to meet on my bed.

And after that we move on. To work, shopping, laundry. To meetings and demos and empty sheets of paper.

Sometimes, this movement against forgetting takes all the courage I have.

Breath

LIKE BREATH I have held you inside of me.

Long days of working   a spring that weeps with delay   bare
maple branches outside my window taut with wind   Your breath
inside me all those days.

Memory: your wide green eyes after we make love   *Touch:* your
hands smoothing my shoulders the day I come back from my
father's frail hospital room   *Sound:* your voice saying I'm *here*
when I ask you on the phone if you're there.

And my body tight when I remember sometimes that your
breath   your voice   your touch are not for loving only me.

In the middle of the night I am frequently fighting: hands pushing
me   pulling me   stealing my childhood away   Morning
comes coldly and slowly   wanting a touch that is giving not
taking   that is womanly and only for me.

When I am reminded of the bare aching fact of me and you and another woman   when I am haunted by memory of me and my father and my mother under one roof   a knife finds its way down my throat.

Then I want everything to be separate   but then nothing is separate: the knife   those hands   my body   your breath the fact of our fragmented love.

I love you in gasps   you love me in long sweet breaths through your lips to my body in a rhythm that rocks me to sleep.

Will this writing be the knife again   breaking branches grafted so newly so tenderly? Knives can pare too   clean   cut away old growth   I imagine a wholeness   I imagine us   although no one else has   I trust in the work we will do together   Sometimes I close my eyes   see a breaking   open my eyes and see: nothing has broken   you were gathering branches while I slept.

In between the hands and the knife I dream about gardens: roses   lobelia   irises   lilacs   and herbs   Words land like birds released from a chimney   The words are beautiful   jealous   patient   and angry   They fly through the garden in order or in chaos   doing their necessary work   The words reach to the ground   heal old roots   a work we are doing together   This work can be pleasure you say.

Lately I've imagined: my own hands pulling the knife from my heart   Or watching it: a probing and paring I can control.

Vancouver Public Library
Central

Check Out

04:34 PM   09/01/2009

1. Comfort food for breakups : the memo
31383081206214   Due: 09/22/09

2. The Vagrant revue of new fiction /
31383081472915   Due: 09/22/09

3. The children of Mary : a novel /
31383081152178   Due: 09/22/09

4. The woman who loved airports : stori
31383047090876   Due: 09/22/09

Total 4 item(s).

Patron Information:
(0 Holds Ready to Pick Up)

Items due by closing on date shown

For Renewals, Due Dates, Holds, Fines
Check your account at www.vpl.ca
or call Telecirc - 604-257-3830

Please retain this receipt

For now nothing has broken   Much has grown in the night
while we slept   legs   arms tangled like tree roots   Roots
come together in time or they don't   Still they grow.

Like breath I will hold you inside of me.

My Skin, Her Skin

MY SKIN: white. No, olive-coloured now, at the end of summer, three months of hot weather bringing melanin and old ancestral skin tones to the surface, giving me what Western culture calls a 'healthy look,' incidentally making me vulnerable to skin cancer too.

I'm working on my tan   I would say to her, jokingly.

Oh *good*   she'd reply, ironically.

Her skin: firm, brown, textured. I wanted to taste every inch of it, I wanted to breathe all its smells. We would argue or be uncomfortable, there would be dishonesty or mistrust, but then there was her presence   my attraction   our difference   making me fall into her body gratefully, thirstily.

My skin: white   pink   hairy   different from hers. She wanted to take me in restaurants or at meetings, telling me later, while we lay in bed. She wanted the difference   she wanted its power.

And sometimes she just wanted: me. And sometimes I just wanted: her.

There are places on my skin that can't be touched at random, like territories on maps with undulating but inevitable boundaries. With someone new to my body, I push the hand away, gently, send it to a different, more generous place.

The nights are full of memory. A certain angle of caress and night pulls backwards into aching. Even my own hand. Self-hatred lives in my skin too. I seek out difference even when it is difference that touches me raw.

Her skin was scar tissue turned hard. Like me, she had her reasons, reasons itemized again and again, pulled out and remembered.

Don't touch me   she'd say sometimes. I am going to touch *you.*   It was sexy but it was serious too.

My skin: reassuringly normal out on the street.

Her skin: abnormal, remarkable, children nudging each other, even in her own neighbourhood. Slogans, chants, assumptions: *le Québec pour Québécois. . . . Pure laine. . . . Immigrants hors d'Québec.* Chased at night. Because of the culture, because of her skin. Police violence, murders. Because of skin.

So we walked on the street together and we became each other's other. We carried history in our skins and we carried it to our bed.

We always turned off the light before making love.

In broad daylight, we sometimes talked. Trying to find the space between: her oppression   my privilege. My ethnicity   her race. And what we had in common: *woman   allophone   activist lesbian.* Or maybe I imagined that we talked. Maybe we didn't and couldn't because no one around us was talking this way and we were living inside an outdated black and white film.

Then I tried to cross the boundary of my white skin. Fell into her skin   abandoned my own. Gave without asking for anything back, until it was too late.

My skin became a symbol   inanimate. Became what she saw: the skin of the white policeman   the skin of the suspicious white children.

Because of her skin, because of my skin, she left. Whose fault was it? I had already abandoned myself.

Years passed. She grew with love and so did I.

I went inside my history and saw what had been done to my own people and what my people had done to others. There was no place to go but home. She knew this too.

History inscribed itself on our bodies in different and uneven ways: *December 6th   Oka   the Gulf War.* The space between her body and mine grew larger. Silence grew in this space like a weed.

I would like to say: that guilt gave way to anger and then to recognition. That, huddling in front of TVs for a glimpse of casualties, in different rooms and cities, reaching out to our own for solace at marches and rallies, we found a common language. Bombing diagrams presented like weather maps. Media like propaganda. Days of unexpressed rage like blank grey eyes. I want to believe that rage took root and grew into action.

Sometimes it did and sometimes it didn't.

I want to imagine: silence giving way to speech. A language that excavates history   that says finally   skin is a myth. That says divided we are lost.

To find the common language between her skin and mine.

Who Do You Think You Are

I HAVE A GOLD brocade top I wear sometimes when Mama isn't looking. Baba made it for Mama and now it fits me like a glove.

I live alone but Mama still looks at me with that look she has. Through the windows, through the phone, she still gets in, her voice crackles snaps me to attention: *Who do you think you are?*

I wear the gold brocade top with my black lace bra, cleavage swelling shyly through the low scoop neck that Baba made for Mama in the 50s when Mama was beautiful but safe: married to my father, the handsome but penniless refugee.

I wear my lace-trimmed panties and my miniskirt, sheer black stockings and simple shoes. I slick my hair back, make a gash of red across my mouth, kohl my eyes, run my hands across my gold brocade breasts, look in the mirror and say: Who do you think you are?

I don't recognize myself when I dress like this and then, on the other hand, I do. A little gold-party-dress-girl, in my memory she's chatty and bratty, she always wants her girlfriends to come home with her, she always wants to wear her yellow organza dress out to play. Round about grade one, she stopped smiling for the pictures. Round about grade seven, she stopped being chatty. Round about grade eleven, she started wearing big tent dresses, she stopped eating. In university, she was the one in men's vests that hid her fine round breasts, the breasts she never looked at, the cunt she never touched. The body she never fucked with, an outline for her soul, that's all she figured it was.

Mama used to wear such beautiful dresses, I've seen them in the home movies. Some of them still hang in her closet, smelling of mothballs and confinement. The summer frock with the orange flowers and tight bodice; the green brocade sheath with the slash down the side, the one I pretended to wear when we played cocktail party in the backyard. The little floral top with the tight red capri pants; the clothes Baba sewed with material on sale at Eaton's, two continents and three decades away from the village she still called home.

Mama had dark curly hair and a red rosebud of a mouth. I have a picture of her as a girl, standing in a prairie field with three other girls. People always find me in that mouth, that picture, that sly femme smile.

So I wear my gold brocade or my polka dots or my silk blouse over my black satin bra while I'm enjoying the curve of a woman's face or the deep notes in her voice. As I lean against the bar with my black leather jacket over my white satin bustier, I like to chat her up and make her laugh. Make a woman laugh, you see her body relax, her shoulders ripple with pleasure, you hear all the notes in her voice. That's how I got my chattiness back.

My body came back in pieces. My breasts when a woman straddled my stomach, dipped her fingers into a glass of wine and tempted my nipples with her dripping, teasing fingers. My stomach when a lover, attentive with longing, waited the long months until she could finally touch the round soft places that used to hurt whenever anyone ran their fingers down. My cunt when a woman stroked me, coaxed me, haunted me with loving butch fingers, insisting and carrying on, kneeling over me and watching me closely, solemnly, as I came. My legs when I put my stockings on, my legs in my short skirt, my legs wrapped around a woman's large ass. My breasts when I touch them, rub them against a woman, roam them against her cunt. My mouth on a woman's tongue, biting, sucking, pulling, teeth along a nape of neck, lips along the inside of a woman's thigh.

I have Mama's voice and lips now, and her gold spark igniting on friction, crackling attitude. And that brocade top I wear with leather jacket proper attitude: femme hot smartass lustiness burning from inside.

Cross-Country Breakup

FRIENDS make me dinner like there's no tomorrow   phoning
long-distance like there won't be no phone bill   and working the
time zones   Vancouver   L.A.   Berlin   Susan in the Kootenays wakes up at seven and puts in the call   Mama makes perogies in Ottawa   Sheena in Montreal brings cookies at two
scotch & Oprah at four   the news the national the local   we're
talkin' major heartbreak and it's not even over it's hardly begun
Sleepytime tea brings no sleep no solace   revenge by night
saccharine forgiving letters by the bleary light of dawn

Everyone's an expert cuz everyone's been there   it's all cheatin'
hearts & trashy behaviour   we're talkin' fear   talkin' patterns
talkin' smalltown betrayal & bigcity gossip   talkin' love as big as
my two arms stretched wide and hurtin' as bad as a C&W song
or as tacky as two women can do to each other & themselves.

What are you doing for yourself asks Susan the social worker
bad food & TV   affirmations & coffee   Chinese herbs   vita-

mins   24-hour Roseanne   candles & remorse all over the
house   Gotta get through my life or at least past the weekend
wanna call 'n say in all languages *basta* enough *ça suffit*   wanna
be all coolness and butch hard   say *baby you're herstory*   but
hope gags my anger and I can't manage either   like watching a
slow-motion accident   you can't stop it can't help it you can't
even scream.

Won't let her go without a good goddamn fight   don't let each
other leave without a good final fuck   sex the last time is under-
water deep & frightening and wise to each other's bodies we come
huge & painful through tears   *you know me so well* she says   *I
felt like your hand went right through me* I tell her   and for the
next month I breathe desperate into & out of that opening now
closing knowing wound/hole.

Heart   lungs   skin   pumping blood & grief from the inside
out   Maybe I'll learn something wonderful & huge I say in a letter to Kathleen but for now it's a grim unlearning   In my 20s I
thought everything added onto everything else   but deep into
my 30s seems like some things take away and never give back
Her gone to another woman feels like part of me erased but I look
in the mirror see me   I'm still here   I think   *baby the part of
me you've erased is really a part of you.*

Today Life Is Like This

Said the earnest little girl to her mom in the pizza place on St. Laurent where we were today.

Today it is raining and we walk anyway   you are visiting from Ottawa and everything is novelty   *frites avec mayonnaise* on St. Denis   the fresh-baked croissant I get for breakfast   my lesbian friends and their loose laughing ways   You have known me since childhood and we can speak in code   Ukrainian for gossiping about the misogynist gay bookstore owner right there in his store or for words we wouldn't couldn't dream of translating Expressions that fit skintight   uttered in the middle of brunch so we're smirking and none of my friends know why   a history that goes back further than our shared 20 years.

You have been in my life longer than any lover will   Your mother my parents are ill   you have been there and been there over the frail long-distance line and now here in my home   Seems like no one else understands how a parent in a hospital bed sends shock

lines of grief through sleepless nights and then outward into daytime life straining to breaking the delicate safety net of community
and love   *Where are my friends where was my lover* we ask each
other then one of us will cry while the other pours wine and we
make each other the most wonderful food.

Yesterday life was like this   it's Easter and friends pour into my
apartment for labour-intensive East European food   we eat and
tell jokes until our stomachs are sore   You decide we should all
make *pysanke*/Easter eggs and nobody thinks they can but we do
until evening and it's time to make dinner   Someone goes to the
dépanneur for more wine   I light more candles because the ones
from this morning have burned down to nothing   you make
Spanish tortilla   I put on Cape Breton fiddle music   someone
starts playing the spoons and my house is full of flowers and
pysanke and women I love   *Takhe zhyttia*/that's life as we say
tomorrow may be different but yesterday filled a place gone empty
and aching   and today life is like this   generous and still.

The Shadows of Your House

THE HOME MOVIES flicker vivid and silent and so were you most of the time   you had a voice then   you often chose not to use it   I lived in terror of your silence   to this day a meal without conversation makes me not want to eat at all.

And now you've lost your voice   now you're trying to get it back   and none of us can even remember how it used to sound.

The year you were ill   days went by like unread pages in a book   days when I didn't use my voice at all   then when I did it was different: smaller   I spoke into my writing I spoke through my work or I didn't speak at all   anyways, for so many emotions there are no English words.

A few months ago I tried to tell you I'm lesbian   *not now* you said and left the room   The next day I was sitting beside your hospital bed   anaesthetic settled like warm water over your body and you smiled as I have never seen you smile before.

I want to go to Thailand you said sleepily out of the blue   okay we'll go together I said   I held your hand.

After the operation you couldn't remember what you'd said and I did not see that smile for a long time.

You were brave everybody said so   you couldn't talk for weeks   we had witty conversations through your notebook   you were more chatty more girlish with your pen than ever with your voice.

The worst time for you was after the radiation   your body pale and limp bludgeoned by toxic rays   Sadness filled the house but so did truth   *I've had a lot of time to think* you said   *my priorities have changed   things that used to make me mad seem unimportant now*   you cried a bit   I wanted to ask: what priorities but didn't   I wanted to hold your hand   but didn't.

The worst time for me was after my lover left   *why aren't you hungry* you asked   words were rocks in my mouth   gently slowly you put food on my empty plate   you had nothing to give but you gave what you had   You became a mother   I became a daughter   everything we needed was in the circle we formed.

Lately you've had a voice again   a temporary synthesized voice grafted through a tube   This voice grows stronger and louder and the more your cancer heals the more your anger seems to return   We argue like we used to before you were sick   stupid things: my haircut   clothes   whose turn it is to call.

Maybe you fear a loss of caring   the warm water wash of support   you allowing it for the first time   trickling away as you
become well.

Maybe you fear your own power   flickering more vividly than
ever in all the shadows of your house.

I'm praying for you you say to me.

Lately I've started singing again   just for myself   the old
Ukrainian songs while doing the dishes or washing my hair   and
I realize I hadn't been singing for a long time.

Map

ONCE, a woman brought a map to the bed we had shared for the
night   asked me to show her exactly where my parents were
from   I traced my finger past wavering borderlines   through
blue-green Carpathian mountains along familiar-looking names:
the town my father was born in   the area on the Polish border
my mother is from   I could feel this woman wanting me to say
the names of towns and villages   wanting to hear the rolling R's
and stretched-out vowels   wanting that sound.

I couldn't say the words   No one   lover or friend   had ever
asked me this before   Moment made me foreign and more
known.

A complicated journey: to find recognition in a lover's eyes   I
become a little girl in ethnic costume performing for a crowd   I
become a woman grown into her history   I become what this
woman needs   to make her story large.

Always to travel: backwards and forwards   stitch the memories
the stories the past and the present together   Then to translate:
this song means this   that expression means that   and finally
to edit out: nightmares of war passed on like old forbidden photographs   Or the gap between the generations   a space as long
and large as an ocean and deeper than years   A space that leaves
no foothold and nothing to say: *this* is how you must live.

Once, I played some old Ukrainian songs for a lover   a Sunday
morning we were poaching eggs in my kitchen it was sunny and
fine   I began to cry when my favourite *"Nich Yaka Hospode"*
came on   why are you crying she said   because it's so beautiful
I said   She nodded: worried.

So many times I've translated words or emotions for lovers
built a vocabulary   *moia lyubov*/my beloved   look I'll show
you where I'm from   Did so because there's no other way   the
language of love is original language   mother tongue.   Found
a new lover started again   became foreign to myself   sought
language again.

Vidchuzeliasia krainia do samohu krayu   my mama used to say:
the country is foreign even to itself.

This was the first time someone said: show me.

But this map is too huge   too heavy   for this fragile temporary
bed.

Enemy Aliens

1. Highway 6, May

DRIVING BACK from Kaslo in Helga's souped-up van: feet on the dashboard   Lillian Allen turned up loud   dub poetry splashing up against big scenery and life feels *fine.*

"I think those are old concentration camp buildings,"† says Helga suddenly, matter-of-factly. "I can tell by the windows. My mom was in a building like that one, over at Lemon Creek."

We drive in silence for a while. The mountains soar blue into blue. *You who know what the past has been,* says Lillian . . . *you who see through to the future. . . .*

---

† Between 1914 and 1920, some 9,000 Ukrainian Canadians were interned in hard labour camps across Canada under authority of the War Measures Act. In 1941, the same Act was used to forcibly evacuate and intern over 20,000 Japanese Canadians.

"There's this look my father gives me," says Helga. "When I was little I always thought it was my fault. . . . "

. . . *and mek we work together,* sings Lillian.

2. *Lemon Creek, June*

Walking the railroad tracks that slice through the Slocan Valley, late afternoon sun moving across old green mountains. There's a sudden coolness on my skin. I pick up an orange stone; it's warm, it holds the heat and I think: it holds memory too.

Up ahead is a rundown building where they put the Japanese in the 40s. Edgewood and Vernon, a few hundred kilometres west, are where they sentenced Ukrainians to hard labour during the First World War. *Enemy aliens.* The words are sore in my throat.

I stand on the tracks   hold the stone with both hands   imagine the hot trains that carried these aliens: bewildered women men and children. I almost see them by the Slocan River where Japanese men would have fished, or at Lemon Creek: women washing clothes in the rushing water while children played.

This part of the country is full of old ghost towns and sudden mists that catch you unawares.

3. *Spirit Lake, July*

Fields of rye blow rivers of green in an uncertain wind. Meadow slopes tenderly down to a lake holding blue reeds and bulrushes, cupped in the curve of its circle. It is too beautiful here.   It is too silent here.

Monastery building squats where the guardhouse once stood. The monks have burned down most of the camp buildings   internment photos have strange prominence on their walls. Frère Roger is hearty but his eyes are cold: *There is nothing to be ashamed of. We're proud of this history. These foreigners cleared the land for us. The Ukrainians in this region, they sing so beautifully, they do those dances and they have those churches, you know, the ones with domes in the shape of a woman's nipple.* He laughs.

At sundown we go to the old camp cemetery, led through the forest by a young girl from town. *Bien, c'est spéciale,* she says when we ask her what she thinks of this history. Ten minutes of blackflies down a boggy unkempt trail, and finally we see it.

Nineteen rotting wood crosses overgrown with lupins and grass. One tall stone cross overseeing them all. A sign that tells the what but not the why and worst of all, it disappears the name of my people. *Ici restent des Austro-Hongrois,* it says.

In five years the crosses will be decayed and gone. There is no time for tears or even a prayer to whomever might be listening. The flies are getting worse   the kid needs to get back and we leave.

The next day photos wheedled from the town archivist speak what the monk wouldn't and the graveyard can't. Thin prison coats in a 50-below winter. A line of men like ants in snow, hauling wood across the lake   young Slavic faces gone stiff with humiliation and cold.

Of course there were Indians here before the missionaries came and disappeared them too. Someone tells us they named the lake after a spirit they saw in the shadows of the water.

But the water is silent   the country is mute and stones do not speak. There is only the barely discernible sound of spirits, pondering:

How history has an insistent repetitive beat   how memory fills the air like mist, concealing and revealing   how we must constantly forget and constantly remember in order to survive.

Finally: A Speculative Tale

Some women wait for change and nothing does change. Other women change themselves. . . .

AUDRE LORDE

1.

SHE WAKES UP with the word *finally* on her breath.

New Year's has just passed and instead of going to a lesbian potluck dinner, which would have been like a psychological laboratory because most of her ex-lovers would be there, she stayed home and added up her losses and her gains on a pocket computer. The computer, which also functions as an address book, social agenda, lesbian film data-base and Christmas card list, is a gift from her new girlfriend (stolen from her last office job).

Losses: Her girlfriend lost her job. So have three million other Canadians this past year: government cutbacks, the latest free trade agreement with Japan, the usual things. Her friend Greta lost a breast. Her ex-lover Celeste lost her unemployment insurance, after being caught at an anti-cutbacks demo. And she, herself, has lost some of her ambitions. Oh well.

Gains: the woman in her bed, after weeks of celibacy. The new winter coat in her closet, bought with leftover money from her last Canada Council grant, just before the Council was dissolved. (The drycleaning bills will definitely be a loss but what the hell.) Gays in the military, free-standing abortion clinics? Her friend Roberta, who reversed a trend and moved to Montreal from Toronto? (Still in denial about the weather here, Roberta 'drops by' for scotch in the middle of a blizzard.) The newly written film script, sitting like clean laundry on her desk? (Nobody funds feminist films anymore, but she'll see.) And then there's her teaching job. Finally.

She always thought she would teach. Almost everyone who has been an artist this long thinks that. Brutal grant cutbacks or unimaginable anti-obscenity and anti-art laws are looming in the rain clouds and everyone's looking for cover. Lots of people think a teaching job – an office lined with books; jovial, tweedy co-workers; respectful students chatting about their required readings; a tidy cafeteria – would be just the thing.

Her office is a dim, airless cell shared with 35 other underpaid part-time faculty. They glare at her with suspicion. Since that guy shot down 30 lesbian students at the university in Toronto last year, everybody's scared. She's teaching lesbian studies. Her students are diffident bar dykes, with backwards baseball caps and purple Doc Martens, who know she wouldn't penalize them for a late paper if her life depended on it. They don't read but their papers are full of charming references to dysfunctional families and lesbian lifestyle lore, which they expect will win her over, and it does. There is no cafeteria, just a dusty bank of sandwich, chocolate bar and coffee machines. There are no staff parties, no colleagues. There is only Bob.

Bob has taken her under his wing. Bob hired her, Bob could hire her again. Bob acts kind. Bob wears tweed. Bob. Is gay.

The woman beside her stirs, mumbles: *Mmmphhrggg.* Opens one eye, looks at the digital clock radio. Opens another eye.

"Baby, it's so early. . . . "

"I had a bad dream."

"*Oomphrggmggrogg.* . . . What about?"

"Bob."

The woman reaches over and pulls her back into the folds of the bed with long, warm arms.

"*Oh, baby.*" They sleep some more.

Finally, last September, it seemed there was a way for lesbians and gay men to work together. There she was, co-teaching lesbian studies and co-programming a lesbianandgay film festival. With gay men. Robert and Bob.

"*Bloody hell,*" exclaimed Roberta over the phone. "Why are you teaching with a *dude?*" Roberta had spent most of her life in kick-ass Toronto cowgirl feminist collectives. She called all men dudes, straight or gay.

"Well, it was Bob's idea. I mean, he founded the course. Like, I get to research all the readings 'n stuff. But he's gonna teach in areas where I don't have expertise."

"Like what? Drag queens? Madonna? Male appropriation?"

"Well, for instance, he's gonna cover the Weimar Period, he knows a lot. . . . "

"Why don't you tell him to talk about the *Wiener* Period? I bet he knows a lot about that."

"Oh, Roberta. This isn't Toronto, you know. We don't have lesbian guerilla vigilante groups here, you know. Things are a little different. A little behind, maybe, but at least you can get wine and beer in the corner stores."

"*Bloody hell.*"

Lesbianandgay film festivals have taken over the nation. They occur at Cineplex Odeon theatres. The merging of the three words – lesbian and gay – is no typo: this is the new corporate name for a culture that sees difference as something that gets in the way of marketing. Occasionally, the term is lesbigay – more popular in the States than in Canada. Like Cineplex Odeon itself, the festivals are all part of one corporation. Every festival shows the same films, which naturally streamlines booking procedures and artist procedures. There are three or four major festival stars each year, who travel together in a rented van to each event, introducing their films. (In the States, they are escorted by gay soldiers and travel in a camouflaged jeep.) With these savings, the festivals spend their extra revenue on larger cinemas and quirky sideshows, like lesbianandgay home video porn contests or decadent swimming pool parties for wealthy queer patrons.

She has a part-time job programming the Montreal Cineplex Odeon *Festival Lesbiennetgaie.* It's a plum job. She works full-time hours alongside Robert, who works part-time hours in his full-time job as president of the festival. She's good at research, so she presents Robert with information about films and filmmakers. Robert usually nods his approval.

They often go to the bar after work. Usually, it's a gay bar, because Robert feels uncomfortable in lesbian bars, sees them as unnecessarily separatist. Also, the gay bars are bigger, with free snacks at happy hour.

"Those separatists are *soooo* stingy," says Robert while she, mouth full of free blue corn nachos, nods her head. The gay bars also have added attractions, like Jacuzzis and steam baths. And the drinks are only $10 each.

She wants to try something new and daring this year: a gathering, an informal discussion, for lesbian filmmakers. A chance to talk about lesbian spectatorship theory, the latest censorship initiatives, the repression of the lesbian gaze, that kind of thing. They've gone to Bar Gros-Cock to discuss her idea. There's some kind of tension between her and Robert today, rising like a summer haze. She buys Robert a double scotch, asks him about his health, gives him a quick shoulder massage when she returns from the can. Robert's been HIV for about eight years and when he gets moody like this, she figures it's because he's contemplating something Big and Complicated, like Life or Death.

Gay men are so angry these days, she muses. They're angry for all the obvious reasons, like that their friends are dying or they are dying. They're angry because, years ago, queers fought for things like gays in the military instead of addressing the fact that the military took money away from saving gay men who were dying. But there is something else to this anger. It's an anger of loss. And the loss isn't just about life. It's about the loss of a *privileged* life. Being white and male is supposed to mean power and respect. Guys like Robert feel they've missed out on some big inheritance. These days, they're getting angry at lesbians, because at least dykes could be giving them some of that power and respect – and dykes aren't coming through on the deal. Dykes, the younger ones at least, want even more of the things gay men want and that just isn't fair.

"Girlfriend, I've been thinking."

"*Mmmhmmh?*" she says, mouth full of free escargot. If she eats enough snacks, she'll be able to skip dinner and recoup her losses on the drinks tab.

"Girlfriend, why do we need to have a silly thing like a girls' discussion group anyways? It's so *borinnnnggg*. They had a girls' tea party at the L.A. Festival and in Berlin they're doing a girls' track meet during the festival, with *cute* things like Broadjump and Dildo Relays, and boys are allowed to watch and it sells tickets. I'm just worried we'll *alienate* people and that would just be *soooo* boring, hon'. . . . "

She nods her head and grabs a plate of roasted eggplant purée, floating past on a silver tray carried by a waiter/drag queen. Out of the corner of her eye, she notices one of her students, unmistakeable in a baseball cap with a *Feminism Works!* logo. Young women wearing these caps are getting bashed by gay men lately, so this woman – Rosallee? Rosemary? – is making a bold statement. She gets distracted by the woman's penetrating gaze and can't hear Robert anymore.

The woman beckons to her, motioning to the alleyway outside the bar. Snatching a basket of basil-parmesan focaccia from a neighbouring table, she follows, as though hypnotized.

2.

Her name is Rosa. À la Luxemburg, of course, that courageous socialist-feminist who ended her days drowned in a river. This Rosa possesses a different kind of courage, rash with youth yet shrewd in a way that isn't young at all. With a mixture of fascination and relief, she wonders: what makes these women willing to fight so much, and is it really worth the stress?

"Look, I've been watching you," Rosa says.

All her students watch her, using peripheral vision to enormous advantage, at the bar on Saturday nights. She can't remove her dates' T-shirts anymore, during her favourite golden oldies tune,

"Everybody's Free." Why does freedom have such a nostalgic sound? Why doesn't she feel free anymore, at the bar or in the classroom?

"I have a plan," Rosa continues. They go off to Bar Isis and Rosa tells her all about her big ideas. Of revenge.

3.

January melts into a brown and slushy late February, and she and Bob are in trouble. On March 8th – the date women formerly celebrated as International Women's Day, now known as Gender Equality Day – she wants to show some international, archival lesbian-feminist films: *Just Because of Who We Are, Place of Rage, Susana, Twin Bracelets.*

"It's not pedagogically sound," says Bob, over cappuccinos in his office suite. "A class like that will create an inaccurate privileging of feminist discourses which have never been positioned within the lesbian canon. Moreover, the men in the class will feel displaced, targeted somehow. Which could be dangerous: remember what happened in Toronto. And it will be historically disjunctive. Besides, it'll make us overbudget."

But she has done her research, has deals from distributors, favours from friends.

"Well, do what you think is best," shrugs Bob.

That week, Bob writes to the department head, telling him in great and exaggerated detail about her plan. The department head is shocked, of course, and fires a memo back, vetoing the idea completely. Bob shows her the memo, apologetically, sadly. Offers to buy her lunch. She declines. She has never before declined lunch with Bob.

In no time, she switches the screenings to Rosa's studio-loft, midnight of March 7th, after class. Rosa's place is womon-only space – Rosa isn't a separatist, she just can't cope with testosterone in her loft, the ventilation isn't so good. Men, including Bob, can't come. She's regretful about this with Bob but there's really nothing she can do.

Teams of women fan out across the city, postering for the event. A truck equipped with loudspeakers, playing k.d. lang's theme song from "Even Cowgirls Get the Blues," cruises around town, dropping flyers. Roberta dons a pink tuxedo and leaflets a few sub-urban shopping malls, just to get a good mix. The *Soir* tabloid does a big feature article, with a cover photo of Rosa draped in cel-luloid, and nothing else.

Sensing the event will be a big hit, Bob offers to book the 500-seat university auditorium for her. Robert and Bob have talked and they think maybe Cineplex Odeon might come through with a deal. Bob hints that a renewal of her teaching contract might be in the works and, by the way, would she let Bob introduce the films?

But Rosa has been counting on the event happening in her loft. She's already arranged for loudspeakers to be hooked up outside the building, for the overflow crowd. It's unseasonably mild for March and women are sure to want to hang out on St. Laurent, what with a dyke-run take-out cappuccino bar just next door to Rosa's building. And Roberta is planning to do her gender-fuck performance piece at the screening.

The event is getting big, bigger than duty or political obligation. It is enlarging into pleasure. It is something to look forward to, something to hang a hope onto or to build an idea from. And that is becoming necessary. Finally.

4.

It's late March and spring is on its way. You can tell by the smell of dog shit and by all the dykes sitting optimistically outside Bar Amazon, in heavy sweaters and mittens, clutching beers.

A lot has changed since March 8th and a lot hasn't. Rosa is planning to have regular film screenings in her loft.

Cineplex Odeon keeps phoning her and leaving death threats on her machine. Robert is taking her to court.

As predicted, the loft party overflowed into the street. There were dykes in baseball caps, dykes in acrylic sweaters and sensible boots, dykes in fun furs, dykes in lingerie, dykes in sweatshirts and Levis, dykes in rhinestones who looked like drag queens but weren't. Liberty, one of her students, set up a kissing booth on the street. Hélène, who owned the vegetarian café, sold hot chocolate and vegé-pâté sandwiches from the back of a truck. In the loft, slides of famous dyke-feminists, like Marlene Dietrich, Audre Lorde and Emma Goldman, flashed on the walls. Women took their shirts off, as though they were at Michigan, including Greta, who showed off the tattoo placed where her right breast had been. Ricky, who used to deejay for dyke bars before they were all taken over by a Wendy's franchise, brought her CDs and got the loft up and dancing to "Everybody's Free" and "We Are Family" before the movies began.

Bob showed up at intermission and the girls went wild. They tore off his shirt and pulled down his trousers. He slowly removed his boxer shorts to the tune of "Fever," sung by Madonna. He let Rosa kneel in front of him and peel the banana packed inside.

The films went on until 3 A.M. Everyone cheered during the scene where Angela Davis goes jogging in *Place of Rage* and there wasn't a dry eye in the loft after the suicide scene in *Twin Bracelets*.

Afterwards, dancing continued in the street. At 5 A.M., a conga-line of dykes was snaking along the middle of St. Laurent, to the beat of "Everybody Everybody," when they were raided by the cops. Several women got arrested and a few got beaten up. A huge committee of dykes was organizing for the upcoming trial. It was the first time in 20 years there had been any lesbian organizing in this city, and there was talk of continuing after the trials were over.

She goes into class the week after the screening, a little worried, a little proud, a little happy. Bob is teaching tonight's class. The Weimar Period. Something feels a bit off when she walks into the classroom. There's Bob, but he looks different somehow, a little smaller, or maybe it's just that she feels bigger. His posture is different. His eyes are more amused. His moustache looks flatter. His hands are more graceful.

Bob is talking about the Weimar Period as an unusual and important time for lesbian culture. He shows slides of dyke bars, he has interview clips with older dykes, he reads excerpts from poetry, he plays some old German lesbian love songs.

She's sitting next to Rosa.

"This does *not* sound like Bob," she whispers. Rosa smiles, with a huge secret behind her eyes.

She looks again and sees Roberta, grinning at her behind a barrier of masculinity and tweed. She turns back to Rosa.

"Well then, where *is* Bob?"

Rosa simply shrugs and rubs her hands together. And Bob is never heard from again. Although, of course, there is still Robert and Tom and Dick and Harry – and they haven't changed at all.

But the women have changed and that makes all the difference.

MARUSYA BOCIURKIW is a long-time activist in Canadian cultural and feminist communities and a former regional editor of *Fuse* magazine. For the past fifteen years she has published articles and reviews in arts and feminist publications, and in recent years her narrative writing has been anthologized in *Fireweed, Dykewords, Queer Looks,* and *The Journey Prize Anthology.* She has also produced and directed over a dozen videos and films, including *Unspoken Territory, Night Visions,* and *Bodies in Trouble,* which are screened internationally. Her multimedia presentation "Cross-Sexing the Narrative" has recently toured the U.S. and Europe.

Born in Alberta of Ukrainian descent, Marusya Bociurkiw studied at Carleton University and the Nova Scotia College of Art and Design, and has taught film studies at Concordia University in Montreal. She currently makes Vancouver her home.

PRESS GANG PUBLISHERS
FEMINIST CO-OPERATIVE
is committed to producing quality books with social and literary merit. We give priority to Canadian women's work and include writing by lesbians and by women from diverse cultural and class backgrounds. Our list features vital and provocative fiction, poetry and non-fiction.

A free catalogue is available from Press Gang Publishers, 101–225 East 17th Avenue, Vancouver, B.C. V5V 1A6 Canada